Homefall Search

Borders & Five Systems Book 1

Dana Bell

WolfSinger Publications ❧ Brackettville, Texas

5 Systems

Aris *(Arkon's Homeworld)*

Deluth

Los

Pri *(Moon)*
Reptilian Race

Nevis

Igtn

Marllon
Dragons

Zelutha
Sharmaine
Wise Women

Ka

Res

Ladou
Vampires

Henri

1-L

Tak

Mes
Hdln

Vitel

2-L

Charon
Charon Felines

P27-K

B
o
r
d
e
r
s

Borders

Saris

(Saris Homefall)

Tashati
Nebula

Valhalla

Valqurie
(Simean Races)

Friend
(V'ianth & T'ganth Homefall)

Bast (Felcat Homeworld)

Ronia (Talon Homefall)

Tal (Wayas Homefall)

AK-5

Methdone

Erin

Arial
(Shapeshifters)

K5   Zeth

(Jovan Homefall)

5

S
y
s
t
e
m
s

Dedication

Thank you, Heavenly Father for this amazing book.
This is all for your glory.
To my mom for her encouragement.

Acknowledgements

My thanks to those who filmed videos of the monkeys who live in the Cambodia refuge. They were very educational. They inspired my characters who live on two planets.

My thanks to Dave Withe who liked the original Homefall Search story and wanted to learn more about the characters.

My heartfelt thanks to my uncles, aunts, and cousins, all part of a large family, who inspired the clan represented in these pages.

Chapter one of Homefall Search was originally a short story in the anthology Different Dragons published in 2013 by WolfSinger Publications. Many changes have been made to fit the story being told in the novel.

Chapter 1

Snow covered the ground. Harrison Talbot tipped his hat back to scratch his forehead debating what to do. Three days ago, the Rover captain Jehna Talon and three of her animal companions had taken the main trail and gone up into the Ghost Mountains. Granted she hadn't said how long she'd be gone, but still, the sudden weather front dropping a blizzard on the Triple D ranch had him concerned.

"I'm sure she's fine," Molly said from behind him. He turned slightly from the window to look at her. She wore a long brown gingham dress with a frilly white apron over it. "Them Rovers are a tough breed. Besides, she's got them animals to keep her fed and warm."

"All she took was a small pack." He'd watched the woman leave after securing her ship. He'd admired the captain for sensibly taking a thick warm cloak. Her companions on the other hand, and he shivered after all the dark whispers he'd heard about the creatures from Arial, he wasn't too sure about.

In the air above the Rover had soared a red-tailed hawk. He supposed the animal acted as some sort of advanced aerial scout. Loping out in front had been a tan and brown wolf along with a black leopard. He'd longed to ask how they'd come to her, but she must have sensed his question and managed to divert their conversation to business.

"Wonder how the cat is?" Molly muttered, retreating back to the kitchen. His nose detected beef stew and fresh biscuits.

"I'm sure it has plenty of food and water." The Captain's final companion had been a silvery white cat named Crystal who he'd been informed would stay on the Rover ship.

"Dang it," he cursed. He grabbed his heavy woolen coat, shrugging it on over his broad shoulders. "Don't hold lunch for me!" he called to his cook.

"Now you wait just a doggone minute," the rotund woman replied.

He heard shuffling in the kitchen, and some slapping pans, as he pulled on his winter boots. Minutes later Molly appeared with a sack and a large canteen. She handed them to him wordlessly.

"I'll be careful," he promised, grabbing his leather gloves and the offered food. "You tell the foreman where I went and to keep things running smooth till I get back."

"You be careful and take Sandy. He's the best horse for a search."

He didn't really need her advice. But, allowing her to give it anyway made Molly feel important and not just his cook and housekeeper. She'd come to him after the death of her husband of twenty orbits wanting a job and he'd taken her in. Everyone on the ranch loved her.

"I always am," he reassured her.

She put her hands on her ample hips and glared at him. "If'n the Rover had been a man; would you go searching?"

"Since the Ghost Mountains are on my land, yes." Or at least he figured he would.

"Uh, huh." She didn't sound like she believed him. "You watch out for that old dragon."

People still had prejudices about dragons buried deep in some old racial memory. Harrison shook his head. "Not much to worry about there."

"We've lost livestock to it."

"I don't begrudge 'em an occasional meal, Molly. He or she was here first."

"Hummpf." She toddled back to the kitchen.

Harrison took a deep breath before allowing the freezing air to invade the house. He pulled his kerchief over his unshaved face and stepped out into the storm. White whirled everywhere and he blinked. Maybe searching today would be a mistake, yet the vision of the woman shivering, freezing and exposed to the elements spurred him on. He didn't want to answer to her clan chief if anything happened to her.

Fighting his way to the barn, he pulled what he needed from the tack room and saddled up Sandy. He'd been lucky to get the horse since those on Valhalla and Valqurie reluctantly sold their breeding stock. The horse had been designed a bit stockier than what he normally rode. Not to mention a thick fur coat, which would protect Sandy from the cold and damp.

He patted the horse's neck. "Ready?"

Sandy snorted his response and the two rode out into the blinding storm.

~ * ~

Freezing wind invaded the small cave where Jehna and her companions had taken refuge from the winter storm. It howled through the canyon outside and pushed brittle leaves into her sanctuary. She began piling them at the entrance, mixing in the thick wet snow, hoping to block out some of the cold.

Hawk perched on a ledge, his russet feathers fluffed out and his head tucked under his wing. She'd never called him anything, but what he was. When he'd accepted her as a travel companion, he'd claimed giving her his name gave her power over him. He didn't want that. She'd graciously agreed although she felt it kept a barrier between them.

Tanner, the wolf, and Dannon, the leopard, had had no problems giving her their names. They joyfully walked beside her as full companions. They'd had many, many cycles of adventures together and would soon embark on a new chapter, if the valley proved acceptable, of their shared lives.

If Uncle Daniel could get the Rover clan leaders to agree, and if she could find enough of her cousins to join her. She might have to reach out to the other clans. Not something generally done. The importance of starting a new Homefall overrode custom.

"Wish the storm hadn't started." She rubbed her hands together and pulled them back under her cloak, thankful the hood covered her dark brown hair. Tanner tugged at the fabric, trying to pull her away from the entrance.

'You'll freeze', he told her.

"All right, I'm coming." She retreated as far as she could inside the small space. Jehna didn't dare start a fire because the smoke would suffocate them all. Dannon growled, pacing. He didn't like being confined. "Easy, Dannon. We have only to wait out the storm."

'Should have moved ship,' he grumbled.

"I'm not making any profit on this trade." She had to ration her fuel. "I agreed to drop supplies for the Triple D in exchange for the right to hike the Ghost Mountains."

Dannon already knew that. She'd discussed the agreement before they'd landed. The Arial tended to think more as the animals they shifted into rather than the intelligent lizards she knew them to be. They didn't live in their ruined cities anymore. Their civilization had declined. Probably the main reason they'd agreed to allow their planet to be re-colonized by a younger race. If that ever happened.

"We'll be setting up the new Homefall in a valley between the ranges. I wanted to get an idea what it would look like and the weather patterns. Make it much easier on the other pilots."

The leopard sneezed and crawled up next to her. She put her arm over his neck. She squeezed briefly before laying down next to him on the hard ground, using her pack as a pillow. He cuddled in close and sighed. Tanner stretched out on the other side, laying his muzzle on her stomach.

Her cloak also helped keep her warm. The snug wrap had been made from spider grass, a rare fabric only found on Sharmain. The Argollian wise women were stingy with their secrets. As one of their blood she had certain rights and her mother had trained her as a healer. Her Rover father had insisted she be allowed to return to the Talon Homefall, Ronia, if she so wished.

She'd done so on her tenth cycle after the death of her mother. Jehna shut down her thoughts. She didn't want to think about it right now. Not when she needed every ounce of her will to survive.

'Still sad,' Dannon whispered in her mind.

"Yes." She closed her eyes and hoped she at least got a nap. Night was coming and she'd doubted the cold would allow her much sleep.

~ * ~

The trail narrowed and Harrison had no idea how Sandy knew where to safely put his hooves. He rocked slightly back and forth in the saddle. The swaying made him want to close his eyes and sleep.

"Stay awake now," he told himself as his breath came out in warm puffs.

Overhead the gray clouds thickened and the snow fell more heavily. He reached up, dumping several inches off his hat. He also brushed flakes off his shoulders. Night approached and he needed to find a secure place to camp. Not just to keep him and the horse warm, but to also have a place to stand against the dragon, in the event they encountered the large reptile.

He didn't actually expect the creature to be hunting in this weather. Most of the sightings, rare though they were, had been during the long summer. His ranch hands had reported odd four or five toed tracks near the corrals. One of them showed him a hard red scale and an odd bristle-like feather.

No one had actually seen or heard the creature.

The horse's head jerked up.

"Easy," Harrison soothed. "Just a bit further."

Shadowy trees brushed his coat. On the other side of the grove there would be a cave they could camp in. Large enough for the horse and small enough to help conserve body heat. Luckily he'd grabbed a warm stone which would help. Worked better than a fire.

They finally cleared the trees and he urged the horse to the side. He'd traveled there many times and knew about the pond on his right and granite cliff on the left. He dismounted and led Sandy into the small cave. He hobbled the horse's front legs, took off the saddle, and gave the horse some oats.

He activated the stone. Heat radiated out and soon the black igneous began to reflect the warmth back. "We'll be toasty here all night," he said, pulling out the food Molly had packed for him. He dined on warm beef stew and a biscuit with fruit jelly. Afterward, he spread his bedroll on the ground and pushed his hat over his closed blue eyes.

Night fell and he slept sporadically. The wind howled outside like he imagined the shifter wolf traveling with the Rover did when the moon was high.

He woke in the morning, stretched and froze.

Regarding him with clear round eyes, was a tiny creature who looked something like a lizard with a red feathery mane around its head. He'd never seen anything like it before. It blinked and scuttled forward, nosing at his food bag.

"You hungry?" Slowly he reached for the bag. The little lizard ducked back, hiding in the shadows. "Shy little guy aren't you?"

Sandy shuffled from one back leg to the other and swished his brown tail. Harrison patted the horse's hindquarter. "You aren't scared of it." A good sign since animals had instincts about what was dangerous and what wasn't.

He hunkered down and pulled out a bit of dried meat. Extending it to his odd little guest, he waited. The creature finally ventured out, grabbed the offering and raced back to safety.

"But you are of me."

Harrison warmed his hands over the stone then ate a breakfast of biscuits and lukewarm tea. As he saddled up Sandy, he watched the spot where the little lizard had retreated. He saw it peek out, look around and then nuzzle up against the stone.

"You cold?"

It raised its head, eyes whirling. For the first time he could see specks of gold and green.

"I'm about to leave and this cave is going to get cold again."

The small reptile put its head back down and shut its eyes. He could see its sides slowly moving and suspected it had fallen asleep much like any baby would after a good meal.

He debated briefly on whether or not to leave it. No doubt it was native to the mountains and knew how to survive. Yet he hated to leave any young thing to fend for itself unless he knew mom lurked nearby.

"You're an idiot," he told himself, even as he pulled an extra kerchief out of his saddle bag. He dropped the fabric on the lizard and managed to bundle it up. It never stirred. He tucked it inside his coat, thankful for all the interior pockets. The creature should be snug and warm there.

"Come on Sandy," he took the reins and replaced the warm stone in the saddle bag. "We need to keep searching."

~ * ~

Dawn crept in and Jehna opened her eyes. Her two companions both stretched their limbs, Dannon arching his back. The leopard washed a spot on his shoulder while Tanner trotted to the entrance and looked out.

'Snow stopped,' the wolf reported.

'Should go back,' the leopard grumped.

"We're almost there." Jehna reached into her pack and pulled out some rations. The roll she selected tasted of cinnamon, raisins and oats. She sipped sparingly from her water container. "If we don't reach the summit today, I promise we'll go back."

Hawk stirred, dumping poop on the rock. He sprang from his ledge and flew out the opening. Tanner leapt outside and Dannon reluctantly followed her into the cold, white world.

The trees sparkled like frozen waterfalls. Jehna gasped in wonder. "It's beautiful."

'My feet are getting wet,' Dannon complained.

Tanner bounded through the snow, leaving a trail for her to follow. Jehna took a deep breath and plunged on, thankful for her fur lined boots. They'd been a gift from her cousin Lon Talon.

What she needed to do was important to the Rovers' future. Too many clan leaders had hoarded their people on their Homefalls after an unknown plague had devastated their numbers about fifteen cycles ago.

Jehna had been a young child when it had happened. Her mother had protected her on Sharmain, but she remembered the wailing as the death toll had been announced. The Rover clans had been hit hard, killing most of the adults over thirty, including Daniel Talon's father, which pushed the young man, only seventeen cycles, into a leadership position before he'd learned all he needed to about leading the clan.

Uncle Daniel had done well though. He'd managed to keep the clan together along with raising several orphaned children. Aunt Taeia, his Argollian wife, had been very supportive and Jehna suspected had been placed in that position by the Arvona herself.

Not that she'll ever admit it.

Jehna knew her aunt well and the policies of the wise women. They stepped in when needed to aid the leadership of any planet or clan.

Unfortunately, their high position in the Five Systems and Borders was a draw for the powerful. The Arkon had claimed the Arvona, her aunt's sister, for his son. Rumors had drifted back from Aris that he'd had the wise woman leader killed after she'd given him a grandchild. A girl of course, not the grandson he craved.

"One day," she muttered under her breath as she followed the wolf, "we'll reclaim her daughter."

'You hope,' Dannon said. Gingerly he put his paw into the snow again.

"We will. There are few who cross the healers who do not pay a high price."

By what she gauged to be midday, they stood on the peak looking down into the valley. A vast expanse spread below them in a field of pristine white. There would be plenty of room to plant crops and possibly an orchard. Meandering along the west edge a wide river emptied into a good-sized lake. Near the north end stood what looked to be an old stone castle.

"Now that's a find!" Jehna couldn't believe her luck. The castle would save a great deal of time and expense. Granted, she had no idea how much repair might be needed, but to already have a place to live was like receiving an approving smile from the All Knowing One.

'Good find', Tanner agreed, his tail wagging wildly. He pushed his muzzle against her leg.

She scratched behind his ear. "Yes, it is." Her sea green eyes drifted upward, taking in cloud formations and making some guesses about wind shear and other factors based on past flying experience. Hawk circled overhead. She sensed his delight as he drifted on the air currents.

'Go now?' Dannon asked, pulling ice from between his toe pads.

Jehna nodded. "I've seen enough to support Uncle Daniel's proposal."

'Good hunting,' Tanner told her. He nosed under the snow and yipped. Rubbing his black nose with his paw he said, 'Odd smell.'

"Well, we don't exactly know what wildlife lives here. Come on," she turned around. "Let's get back to *The Lady*."

Hawk voiced a high-pitched warning. Jehna saw the shadow and instinctively stopped. Dannon and Tanner both growled, crouching down into attack positions.

Before her, as if it owned the mountain, stood a huge, red-plated dragon with a wild matching feathered mane, looking at them with baleful golden-green eyes.

~ * ~

Sandy plodded up the mountain trail. The sun sparkled on the snow and the wispy clouds floated across the sapphire sky. Harrison thought he heard something and pulled back on the reins. The horse bobbed his head as he obediently stopped.

The high-pitched screech repeated itself and he kicked the horse in the sides. Sandy broke into a trot. Although Harrison knew the sound could be coming from anywhere, and even farther away than he thought, he hoped it was closer.

The pair cleared the narrow canyon and beyond he could see several figures near the cliff's edge. Hovering over them stood a huge reptile, which could only be the unseen dragon. Without thinking he yanked the rifle from its saddle holster and aimed at the creature as Sandy trotted on.

"Don't shoot!" the Rover captain yelled.

Harrison hesitated before lowering his rifle. The huge red reptile turned its long neck to look at him. It backed up, its hindquarters bunched as if to run away.

The Rover made a stopping motion with her hand. He reined in the horse and sat watching the scene before him.

Captain Talon slowly moved away from the cliff edge, urging her animal companions to follow her. They both crouched low, ready to spring. The leopard's tail flicked constantly.

After several long heartbeats she stood next to him. Her hand rested on the horse's neck. "We're in no danger."

"It's a dragon." Whatever he might have said to Molly about not begrudging a cow or two, was true. Coming face to face with the monster and not knowing when it would pounce, another.

"It's very shy. It almost ran away when Dannon and Tanner growled at it."

"Why didn't it?" His heart pounded in his chest.

"It's curious."

"No wings." He wasn't sure why he thought it should have them.

She shook her head. "It gets around like a lizard." The Rover pointed at the tracks in the snow.

Like the lizard Harrison had in his pocket. He opened his coat and a small head poked out.

The dragon took two steps toward him, flicking its serpent pink tongue and whipping its tail.

"I suggest you put its young on the ground and then let's get out here."

"Good idea." He removed the lizard and handed it to the Rover captain. She put the youngster on the ground. It swam through the snow and bumped the adult on the leg. Its mother tasted it and then the two vanished into a high snow drift.

"Time to go." Jehna lifted her arms. Harrison helped her mount. She sat behind him and put her arms around his waist. "Thank you for coming to find me." She giggled. "Would be a long cold walk back."

"You're welcome. What were you doing up here anyway?"

"We want to start a new Homefall. The valley below," she pointed with her chin. "Has good potential."

"I own it you know."

"Well, then, you and I have some business to discuss."

Chapter 2

His foreman Donald, a hefty man who could handle a steer almost single handedly, met Harrison at the barn door. The man flicked snow from his heavy coat as he took Sandy's reins and led the group to the horse's straw-filled stall.

Harrison nodded his gratitude, too cold to say anything.

"Best git into the house," Donald advised as Harrison waited for the Rover captain to dismount. "Molly has the fire going and some hot stew waitin' for you. I'll take care of Sandy."

"Thanks." He dismounted, his body shivering. On the way back a storm had caught them in the canyon and he honestly didn't know how Sandy found the way home. "You okay?" he asked Jehna.

"Fine." She brushed snow from her cloak and checked on her companions. The large cat, Dannon she'd called it, seemed unhappy, snarling and lashing its tail. Tanner, the wolf, shook himself spattering snow everywhere. His tail wagged and he bumped the Rover. She gave him a scratch behind his ear. Hawk, still an odd name for the majestic bird, poked its head out of her cloak. Gently she released the bird who took a perch on an overhead beam.

"You don't mind if they stay in here." Her tone didn't seem to be asking. "I'm uncomfortable with trying to return to my ship. Afraid we might get lost."

"Not a problem." Since Sandy didn't seem to mind, he figured it would be okay.

"House is just across the yard." He moved to the door, gritting his teeth. The temperature had dropped significantly and snow fell so heavy he hoped they didn't lose their way.

She nodded, speaking to her companions in a soft singing tongue. The cat and wolf found an empty stall and curled up together, their eyes quickly closing. "The storm exhausted them," she explained.

"Me too. Best grab my belt so we don't get separated."

She nodded. He felt her fingers take hold and he had to push hard to open the door. It slapped shut behind them. Lifting his arm, he pushed across the yard, trying to keep his eyes focused on the faint light coming from the house. Seemed to take them forever to cross the short distance and he breathed a sigh of relief when they reached the front entrance.

"Mercies sake!" Molly cried as he opened and shut the door, dragging the Rover captain inside. "You two look like snow devils!"

No doubt they did. He shook off the snow and put his coat on the rack inside the door. Captain Talon did the same. Odd, her cloak didn't even look wet.

"That fire feels good." She knelt down before it and put her hands close, warming them.

"We'll get you all warmed up," Molly promised. "I'll put dinner on the table." She disappeared toward the kitchen in a flurry of blue gingham.

"Thank you," he muttered. Harrison dared to allow his fatigue to catch up. His whole body ached from the tension of the long ride. He hadn't dared to stop and camp. They would have been stuck on the mountain for days and he knew they didn't have enough supplies to outlast the storm.

"Nice home." The Rover stood, stretching her body.

"Cold doesn't bother you?" His turn to warm his hands. The fire's heat penetrated his fingers and the rest of his body.

"My cloak is pretty warm and I had Hawk's body heat as well."

He had to admit he'd shared some of it. At least his back hadn't gotten cold.

"Dinner," Molly announced, before going back to her domain.

He moved from the main room into the dining area. His home was modest in comparison to some of the other spreads. The table he'd made himself from a stump he'd found in the south pasture. Crafting it had taken him months to make. He sat and waited for his guest to do the same.

She slid into the chair and bowed her head. She must believe in the All Knowing One. He waited until she finished and picked up her tin mug, taking a sip. "I love tea."

"Molly grows the plants in the garden. Mixes her own blend."

"It's very good."

Hot beef stew reached his nose and suddenly his stomach woke up. Taking a spoonful, he tasted the rich flavor, yet knew to eat slow. He buttered a biscuit and spread the fruit jam.

Jehna smiled. "Want to discuss business now or after dinner?"

"Now works."

~ * ~

From what Jehna had seen Harrison Talbot had a more successful ranch than most. Granted some were larger, others smaller, but he had the most land and it seemed odd to her he seemed willing to sell a valley with both water and rich grazing.

She nibbled the biscuit and watched him across the table. Harrison could be considered handsome, in a rugged sort of way. The toll the land had taken on him she could easily see. The slight crinkles around his blue eyes, his calloused hands and the slight touch of gray at his temples.

Her read on him indicated he liked to be upfront. Jehna could do that. "What do you want for the valley in the Ghost Mountains?" Part of her dreaded his answer.

He chewed briefly as if considering his answer. "Credits wouldn't be much good here." He had a point. Out in the Tashuti Nebula regular currency would be useless. Nowhere to spend it.

"Always interested in a good trade." Wouldn't buy her fuel, still she'd been flying long enough to know how to work multi-layered deals so everyone won.

"So I've heard." He bit into his biscuit and chewed as if considering. "Good land you're looking at."

She tried not to smile. He wanted to make a deal and was trying to make it seem like a huge sacrifice, a tactic she knew well. "Agreed."

He glanced at her surprised, not expecting her response. "I have one thing we really need." There always was. All she had to do was wait for him to tell her.

Her host shifted uncomfortably. He took another spoonful of stew and ate it before replying. "Wives."

~ * ~

With the night the wind came howling. Harrison shivered, thankful for the thick curtains over his bedroom windows. Molly had made them. Would help keep out the chill; as would a body sharing his bed. He hadn't had that comfort since his wife had died two orbits ago. Troubled him to think of her being buried under the blizzard raging outside.

Also troubled him he'd been blunt truthful with the Rover captain. Every ranch had the same shortage. Women didn't migrate to the nebula. They preferred to stay on the more settled planets where comforts could be offered.

What did he have to offer? A hard-working ranch, a rough life on the frontier, the pride of being a settler. He doubted many women would want the same.

He remembered the look on Captain Talon's face after he told her. Her expression had been thoughtful. "I may be able to help you with finding wives," she'd replied. "I'll write up the deal when the storm stops and I can get to my ship."

"Fine." He hadn't expected her quick agreement. Still, he had to remind himself the Rovers had a reputation of being shrewd traders. That's why they'd kept the monopoly on the trade routes for longer than anyone could remember.

"I'll have Molly make up the guest room," he'd offered.

"Appreciate your hospitality."

They'd finished dinner and he'd gone out to check on his men and the herd. The stocky cows had pushed against the main fence, using the barn to help protect them from the weather. Donald had already taken the calves and their mothers inside. No need to lose the young ones.

His men mostly had already crawled into bed. A few sat up playing cards, while the wind shook the bunkhouse. They'd given him a nod before he'd fought his way back to the house. Upon his return, he discovered Jehna had retired for the evening. No doubt Molly too had gone to bed. She tended to get up before the sun rose.

Alone in his room, he had too much time to think and miss his wife. The thought of having close neighbors both made him happy and nervous. Would be a good thing to have Rovers on Saris and might make it easier to import the goods needed.

He just hoped he hadn't asked too high a price by requesting wives.

~ * ~

Wives!

Jehna shook her head as she brushed her brown hair. Who would have thought it would be so simple. Granted, might take a bit of doing, yet she knew exactly who to contact. There were always women who wanted to start over and they always seemed to end up at Tamzin's. Some stayed and worked in her brothel, others found employment elsewhere or, in the event of children, the Charon female found homes for them.

The drawback, and Jehna put down the brush slowly thinking about it, was that Tamzin lived on Aris, the home planet of the Arkon himself. She'd have to go into the very heart of the Five Systems and not stay in the comfort of the Borders.

Not that she hadn't lived in the Five Systems before, not with being raised during her youngest years on Sharmain. She knew both well although she preferred to trade closer to her Homefall on Ronia, soon to be Saris, if she could make this deal work.

Rising she dared to look out the window. Nothing but thick white met her eyes. Her fingers traced the fabric. No doubt Molly had made the bright yellow gingham curtains and the thick colorful quilt covering the bed. The room had been brushed white and contained a stump for a nightstand with a small warming stove in the corner.

She wondered where the vanity had come from and frowned, remembering a few details she'd noticed. The most obvious had been a picture on the polished wood fireplace mantel of a man, a younger version of Harrison, and a woman, probably his wife, standing in front of the house. He hadn't mentioned being married and suspected something had happened to her.

Not one to pry she wouldn't ask. Always better when the information was freely offered.

'Always,' a sleepy voice sounded in her mind.

'You should be sleeping, Tanner.'

'As should you.'

'Soon,' she promised, sitting on the bed. The springs creaked. Taking off her black pants and matching top, she crawled underneath the covers and dropped into sleep, filled with dreams of a new life in the valley she'd found.

~ * ~

Morning brought several metras of snow, which the hands had already begun clearing. Harrison knew the rare late season storms sometimes brought more than just rain. He sipped the cocacof Molly had managed to push into his hands, standing on the porch. He grinned remembering how his housekeeper grumbled he should eat before starting a hard day's work.

His stomach growled and he gave in, going back into the warm house. He found his guest already seated at the table, with a cup of tea and a plate full of flapjacks and eggs. Sitting across from her, he reflected how good it felt to have a woman to share his meal with.

"Morning," he greeted.

"Good Morrow," she returned, sipping her tea. "How bad?"

He shrugged. "Been worse. Might be able to get to your ship by late today or early tomorrow."

"Today would be best. Uncle Daniel will be expecting a report."

He'd heard the Rovers had uncles, aunts, and cousins, not always related to each other and found himself wondering how they kept it all straight.

She smiled, her oddly shaded green eyes dancing. "When you're raised around it, doesn't seem strange at all."

"You read my mind." That chilled him. He liked his privacy.

"Not intentionally. Thoughts do leak through." She picked up her fork. "I have a great respect for other's privacy."

"Good to hear." He dug into his breakfast. The food tasted wonderful. Hiring Molly had been one of the best decisions he'd ever made, and he often reminded himself of that.

~ * ~

After breakfast, she waited until Harrison returned outside to grab her cloak and head across to the barn. Molly had given her a basket of meat for her friends. She found them in the same stall they'd slept in, with Hawk now sitting on the fence. He eyed the basket keenly.

"Here." She gave him a long strip of red meat. Taking the food into his red beak, he took flight back up to the rafters.

'Ate mouse last night,' Dannon complained.

"You or Hawk?" she asked, dividing up the rest between the leopard and wolf.

Tanner gobbled his down, licking what he could out of the basket. Dannon took his time, growling every time the wolf tried to steal some. He finally had to swat the other before Tanner took the hint and trotted outside to relieve himself.

She openly looked around the barn. Several stalls had cows with calves in them, others held horses. Walking over to Sandy, she took a moment to study the animal. He'd done well in getting them home and she could see why. The horse was one of the specially designed breeds, probably bought from one of the two worlds who specialized in the process.

"Must have set you back," she said, as she sensed Harrison behind her.

"Worth every credit." He reached over to fondly rub the horse's forehead.

"They allow you to breed?" Sometimes contracts allowed it, other times not. She wondered what the agreement had included.

"Given I'm living in the nebula, yeah, I'm allowed to breed."

"Lucky."

"Yeah." The rancher shuffled uneasily, pushing his hands into his coat pockets. "How long you figure it will take you to locate women who are willing to come here?"

"I know who to talk to." No need to go into detail. The less he knew about how she worked her trading deals the better.

"Need credits to pay for them?"

At least he'd offered. She shook her head. "There are always those who want to start over." She reached up to stroke Sandy's neck. Her fingers sensed the strength in him and the softness of his hair. "Have an age range in mind?" They hadn't discussed too many details the night before. They'd both been very tired. "Youngest hand is twenty orbits. Most have seen about thirty."

Gave her an idea on where to start. "How do you feel about family groups?" Unlikely that might happen, but she wanted to cover all possibilities.

Harrison kept quiet for a few minutes. He probably hadn't thought about it. "How likely you might find one willing to come here?"

"Not very. Just want to have it covered."

"Hard life for children."

"As I said, there are many wanting to start over."

He patted Sandy's neck, giving Jehna a searching look. "I won't ask too many questions, Captain. Only asking you bring as many as you can."

"How many hands do you have?" She'd add one to include Harrison.

"About twenty. Hoping to add to that number."

Meant she should plan for that and bring more than twenty-one. "I have a basic idea on what you want. Women wanting to start over and marry." With Tamzin's help, her task shouldn't be too difficult.

"Pretty much." He leaned on the stall. "How many you planning to bring to start your Homefall?"

"As many as will come."

~ * ~

Her answer told him the risk she was probably taking in starting a new Homefall. He'd heard about the plague which had nearly destroyed the Rover clans orbits back. Fortunate for him it hadn't, since they proved to be the only ones who could navigate the odd eddies and currents of the Tashuti Nebula. He'd arrived on a Rover vessel, along with his wife and five hands, with a few cows and a couple of horses.

He waited briefly before asking. "Personal favor." He held his breath wondering how the Rover would reply.

"Name it."

Harrison hadn't expected her to agree so easily. "Like to have a dog and maybe some cats. The mice are out of control."

Jehna laughed, sounding like wind chimes on a brisk day. "I'll see what I can do."

~ * ~

The contract had been signed and safely tucked into her ship's memory vault. Jehna had been forced to wait a few days due to bad weather before contacting her Uncle Daniel. Once it cleared she'd been able to access her ship, put together a contract both parties agreed on. Then she unloaded a few supplies Harrison mentioned he needed and she'd had in her hold with payment of seeds and cuttings from fruit trees. A good start for her Homefall.

She waved one final time to Harrison Talbot before closing the hatch making a promise to herself she'd find him a good prospect for a wife. The man deserved one. Standing in her control room, her fingers lightly touched the blueish green orb, which rested on a brown stand looking much like a tree stump, its branches twined to hold the globe. It pulsed as her mind connected to it. *The Lady* rose into the air, breaking atmosphere, and she set a temporary orbit instead of heading out into space.

Fortunate the nebula didn't interfere with communications, or at least not for Rover ships. They had a long-standing agreement with the Marllonian dragons, who liked to explore old ruins and make discoveries, to have first access to any technology discovered. Their ships were far more advanced than the Arkon's military.

She smiled as the signal reached Ronia. Her Uncle Jeremy answered. He'd been among the fortunate few who had survived the plague. His craggy face grinned at her as it hovered above the globe. "Ah, Jehna, we were beginning to worry."

"Heavy snowstorm. Uncle Daniel about?"

"He's been waiting." A temporary darkness before it was replaced by Daniel Talon's lean face. His blue eyes lit up when he saw her. "Jehna! Good to hear from you."

"Sorry Uncle Daniel. Weather." She went into detail about the storm and the valley she'd found. Even told him about the local dragons.

"Might interest one of the old lizards."

"I'm taking some scans from orbit. Looks like there might be some ruins."

"Might be a profitable side business."

"Might be," she agreed. Jehna would think about it later.

"So, what kind of price are we looking at?" All business. She expected no less from her clan leader.

"He agreed to trade."

Her uncle frowned, running his hand through his brownish blond hair. "I hadn't expected that."

"Neither had I, but the reason makes sense."

"What does he want?"

"A dog, some cats," she paused for effect. "And wives."

Chapter 3

"Wives?" Daniel whistled. "That's a tall order."

"But not an impossible one."

"You're thinking of negotiating with Tamzin." Her uncle knew her well. He should, he'd raised her after her parents both died.

"Best place to start looking."

"It's going to be hard enough getting enough for a new household." Her uncle stopped himself. "I know, I know. Take your first trade and work from there."

She smiled. He'd remembered the first principle he'd taught her. "Exactly. Let's worry about getting the land, which, by the way has a dwelling already. No idea what shape it's in."

"That's a blessing," her uncle agreed.

"There's also a water source and plenty of room for a landing field."

"Double blessing."

"All the details should be in my report and contract."

"I'll take a look at those as soon as I can." He rubbed his jaw. "Can't believe the rancher was willing to sell via trade."

"As you always taught us, there's always a need that can be filled."

"Speaking of need." His eyes softened. His wife must have joined him. "I know we're not talking about a household yet, but we may have a healer."

"When the time comes, we can talk about it." Jehna didn't want to get too far ahead and make promises she may not be able to keep. Bad enough the clan leaders might shut down any plans for a new Homefall since her uncle hadn't really consulted them about her trip.

He nodded. "How far out are you?"

"You know the nebula." He should as he'd flown it often enough.

"Are you stopping here or going straight to Aris?"

"Think I'll come home first to fuel up, unless Uncle Assar has figured out how to overhaul and install the new system?" She doubted it, yet figured she'd ask anyway.

Her uncle shook his head. "Not yet."

"I'll see you when I land." She cut the communication and stayed at the orb until she'd crossed the nebula border into regular space. Setting her course, she let the ship fly itself before opening the control room door.

Crystal urped at her, daintily strolling down the corridor as if she expected Jehna to follow her.

"Miss me did you?" she asked following.

The silver white cat stopped and blinked gold eyes. Evidently the Felcat didn't feel like talking. She often didn't. One way the feline race of historians protected themselves. Unless they traveled with a dragon then the rules seemed to be different.

Her living quarters were located in the center of the ship. Crystal scampered inside heading straight for her food dish. The ship's system automatically fed the cat, so Jehna had no reason to be concerned. Her eyes scanned the area anyway.

"You have plenty of food."

Crystal sat, her pink tongue cleaning a spot on her shoulder. Her attitude indicated it was more important than food.

With a laugh, Jehna put a kettle on the small burner for tea. Her cooking space had been designed for one person. One day she might think about expanding the area, should she ever find a man she wished to be braided with. Given her current choices, she hardly thought it possible. No one among her cousins interested her and she hadn't accepted any proposals from any of the other clans.

She'd been raised to be the Homefall leader by her Uncle Daniel. She attended the clan chief meetings with him and had followed him around Ronia since she'd been about eleven cycles. Jehna knew how to run a household. She had healer training as well. Her Aunt Taeia had added to her education after her mother's death.

Hard to believe her clan leader's braided wife also served as Arvona to her people. A role Taeia inherited after her sister's death. Unfortunate the one who had the Arvona killed had died. He owed a debt to the wise women.

Taking the hot water and pouring it into a cup, she set her tea to steep.

Crystal hopped up on the crescent shaped blue couch and proceeded to properly wash herself. Must be nap time Jehna mused.

Her eyes scanned her quarters. Smaller than most, it contained the couch, a wall with shelves inset for a few books she had managed to trade for and scattered personal items. A closed door led to her sleeping bunk, large enough for two, if ever needed.

Dannon, Tanner and Hawk liked to roam and sleep in the cargo bays in the lower area of the ship, keeping the space rodent free. They rarely joined her and Crystal.

She finished making her tea and sat down on the couch. The Felcat blinked at her, before closing golden eyes. Jehna sipped her tea, listening and sensing her ship as they headed for home and family.

~ * ~

The Lady slipped out of the space window and eased into orbit around Ronia. Jehna watched the approach in the misty images over the orb. The Talon Homefall sat below. The main household had been built on the largest land mass, spread out on a huge desert. A sparkling lake fed by underground springs touched one side of the compound with tall stone walls surrounding the rest.

Not far away sat a tall stone tower housing the main com center used to direct ships into port. From the number of vessels sitting on the ground, most of the clan had come home. Not too unusual, but enough to make Jehna curious.

"Welcome home," her Uncle Jeremy greeted. His flickering image solidified.

"Good to be home," she replied. "Any reason almost everyone is on the ground?"

He chuckled, rubbing his unshaved chin. "Seems young Adrian might have found himself a woman to share braids."

"Oh?" She knew most of the available women in the clan and doubted any of them would have chosen him.

"She's a Jovan cousin."

Intermarriage among the clans wasn't unusual and she knew of the young woman. Another whose mother had been a Wise Woman and father a Rover and had trained as both. "What's her clan leader's price?"

"Still being negotiated." Jeremy grinned. "Suspect it might be high."

"As a healer, she will have a stronger say."

Her uncle nodded. "Set down wherever you can find an open slot."

"I need to refuel."

"There are a couple spots near the depot. Your choice."

"Thanks. See you on the ground." She cut the communication and guided her ship to one of the open spots, coming in close enough to be refueled. Luckily, they used a nonflammable fuel, unlike some of the Earth colony ships they'd heard about. A few had managed to reach both the Five Systems and the Borders. Their fates she could not be sure of although she'd heard plenty of whispered outcomes.

Exiting her ship, all her companions joined her, Hawk taking to the sky immediately. Crystal sat on Dannon's back. The silver white against black fur gave a startling impression. Tanner loped ahead, jumping up on Ryk Sargol, one of her non-related cousins. The tall older blond man gave the wolf a good head scratch before nodding his head in greeting.

"Hello, Ryk," She knew her uncle had decided Ryk would be among those who joined her at the new Homefall. He had a daughter Tuleh, who would soon be old enough to braid. The girl apprenticed on her father's ship the *Starrite*.

"You'll be heading back out." He matched her stride. His muscular body carried their Homefall colors well, black with intertwined orange and green piping down one arm with a matching one on the pant leg.

"I will. Trading to be done."

"Uncle Daniel is very happy with the contract you negotiated."

"Just following what he taught me."

Her cousin nodded, a touch of sadness still lingering in his gray eyes. He'd lost his wife Mirra a few cycles back and tended to ignore the many attempts of women trying to gain his attention. "You know Uncle Daniel's plans."

She knew what he referred to. "We're free to make our own course."

Ryk frowned. "Uncle Daniel thinks we'd be a good match."

She stopped as the hot wind whipped around them. "I respect you'd make a good second for our new Homefall." Jehna considered her next words carefully. Ryk had mild telepathic abilities. Most Rovers did since they used the power to fly their ships. "I'm not looking to be braided."

He nodded, his expression relieved. "Nor am I. Glad we're

clear."

"We are."

Hawk cried above them, heading for his perch in the small grove inside the compound. Aunt Taeia had planted the trees, herbs and flowers along with building a small stone waterfall, or rather Uncle Assar had along with digging an attached pond. Their clan leader's wife spent much of her time there.

"You're headed for Aris," Ryk continued as they approached the large gate they could close and lock with heavy shields in the unlikely event of an attack.

"Need to broker a deal with Tamzin."

"Given her beliefs in the All Knowing One, it surprises me she runs the most popular brothel in Arkonna."

"She does more as you are well aware."

He chuckled, the light touch of his mind tickling hers before he'd blocked, thus preventing any further contact. His intimate contact hadn't lingered so she wouldn't chastise him.

The gate stood open. She walked inside, trying to ignore the rising temperature. Much of her family hurried about or sat on benches talking with each other, a sight she had committed to memory and carried with her when she traveled.

"Where's Uncle Daniel?"

"Still speaking with the Jovan clan leader."

No doubt the conversation would be a long one. Rovers tended to father male children. Females were prized and the Jovans, she knew, had dwindled as a clan. They would need to ally with others in order to survive. Both the V'ianeths and T'ganths had merged and lived together in their Homefall for a similar reason.

"I hope he's successful." She moved toward the grove wanting to sit in the tree's shadows and listen to the fountain. The trickling water rested her soul.

"If he isn't, Adrian may just go abduct the girl and we know what type of problems might arise if he does." Ryk sounded amused.

"She must be very special to catch Adrian's interest." The young man had apprenticed with the Wellers and after he'd bought his own ship, he still helped them barter trades. Secretly, she hoped the group might join her new household. They'd give her an additional five ships, not just two, making the new Homefall more profitable.

"What are you thinking?" Ryk sat next to her.

The trees cut out part of the sun and lessened the growing heat. "Just thinking like a clan leader and planning for the future."

"You're pretty sure you'll get the land."

"I am." Harrison had been more than willing to trade and the dragons they'd encountered, although she sensed they'd never been in danger from the creatures, made the deal even sweeter. Not many would venture into the mountains for fear of them.

"You're going to be a strong clan leader," her cousin assured her.

"One you'll be able to follow?" She waited for his answer.

"Willingly."

Chapter 4

Jehna lightly knocked on her clan leader's door, waiting for the invitation to enter. Her Aunt Taeia answered, a smile on her attractive face. "Welcome home," she greeted. Today she'd put her light brown hair up, her braid hanging on the left side of her head, bound at the end with a bit of gold metal.

"Good to be home." She stepped inside, the temperature dropping by several degrees. "How's the negotiating going?"

"Your cousin told you." Her aunt closed the door, taking a seat on the white crescent shaped couch. Over the back was thrown a handmade quilt with swirls of blue, purple and green.

"As he should." Jehna joined her aunt on the couch. "So how is it going?"

The Arvona smiled, her pale green eyes sparkling. "Adrian will have his bride."

"I'm sure the story on how they met is…interesting." Her cousin wasn't quite the troublemaker some of the other Wellers had proven to be. Still, for him to select a Jovan woman, there had to be a fun story there.

"I haven't heard." She smoothed her simple green gown. The shade complimented her eyes. "He came and asked Daniel to inquire about the bride price."

"Hope Adrian can meet it." Depending on their standing within the clan, the amount could vary. Granted, it could be paid in credits or trade or both.

"Our men need to start looking beyond the clans to find a bride."

"Like Uncle Daniel did?" Jehna did not miss the look of pain on her aunt's face.

"Daniel is unique," her aunt quietly answered.

Speaking of her uncle, he entered the room from his private com, running a hand through his hair. His braid had the same gold metal as his wife's. He wore the clan colors, with a stripe around his neck to indicate he was the clan chief.

"What did they ask for?" his wife questioned.

"More than they should have. She's a blood cousin, but worth the price as a healer." He offered Jehna a smile. "We're glad you're home."

"Briefly. I'll need to head for Aris as soon as possible."

"You made a good trade." He chuckled. "Luckily it's an easy one to fill." Her uncle took a seat on a wooden rocker he'd made for his wife when their son had been born. "How many?"

"At least twenty-one. He plans to expand, so I might bring more."

"The Five Systems is a good place to start. The Nobles have stirred up trouble and made life for everyone else more difficult." He rubbed his chin. "Might find more than you have room for."

"Perhaps you should take Ryk with you," Taeia suggested.

"I can handle this trade." She didn't want her cousin along. Her aunt and uncle had made their wishes very clear. They'd strongly suggested the two were a good match, making her glad she'd talked to Ryk about their plans and they'd come to their own agreement.

"One of the traits of a clan leader is to delegate responsibility," her uncle began.

"Uncle Daniel, until I'm actually a clan leader, I'm going to treat this as a normal trade."

He narrowed his blue eyes but didn't argue with her. "While you're gone, I'll speak to the clan chiefs."

"Think it will make a difference?" Given the situation, she doubted it.

"Probably not. Still, I will make it clear we are going to start a new Homefall."

"You said something about a possible healer for it?" Jehna knew she wouldn't be able to be both a clan leader and healer. Both required more time than she'd have.

"In route from Sharmain," Taeia said, with a glance at her husband. "Altair Dawne and her daughter Arissa."

"Braided?" If so it could cause a problem.

"No. Her husband died when their daughter was three cycles."

Good. Meant the healer might be able to braid, depending on her age. "We should wait until the land is purchased before we start gathering a clan."

Her aunt lightly touched her hand. "Altair and her daughter want a fresh start. Where better than a new Homefall?"

~ * ~

As Ronia faded behind her, Jehna concentrated on the trade ahead. The stars faded as *The Lady* slipped through the windows, winding a course to the Five Systems and Aris.

'You not happy.' Tanner sounded concerned. 'Trade bad?'

'No. Trade good.'

'Why worry?'

'Clan chiefs council.'

'Your uncle handle. No need to worry.' She caught the image of a large rodent.

'I appreciate your reassurance.' She chuckled. 'Concentrate on your hunting. I hate pests on my ship.'

'Good eating.' The wolf cut the contact, but not before she got a sample of the taste. Good thing Tanner enjoyed his prey raw. She preferred her meat cooked.

With a shake of her head, she returned to her quarters. The journey to the capital of the Five Systems would take at least three days. While traveling, she'd spend time in her cabin, probably reading. Jehna selected a book and sat on her couch, slipping off her boots and curling her legs underneath her.

As she escaped into the adventure, the light touch of a paw distracted her. Crystal gazed up at her, gold eyes meeting hers. "You don't usually ask for attention." The cat bumped against her, settling down against her leg, her pink tongue busy washing the silver white fur. Crystal's body vibrated and Jehna gave the cat a stroke down her back. "There are days I wouldn't mind if you spoke to me."

The Felcat paused in her bathing and blinked, before returning to her task.

"Or not." Jehna sat back and continued reading, her mind and body attuned to every sound and movement her ship made.

~ * ~

Daniel stood in his com room, trying not to lose his temper. Uncle Assar had designed it to contain a chair and desk, with an orb set in a five-pronged metal design. The room itself had no windows so none could overhear or see what communication had taken place.

By far, he was the youngest clan leader, only being about thirty-two cycles. Andron Jovan was older, his stern face glaring at him with disapproval. Digin V'ianeth and Rigon T'ganth looked thoughtful, yet had not voiced their support. Demtrie Wayas, standing in for his clan leader whose wife was in labor, rubbed his wrinkled face and nodded as if the decision was a forgone conclusion.

"We have to expand if we are to survive," Daniel repeated. How many times had he told them the same thing? He sat in his chair trying to get more comfortable since his back had been hurting most of the day due to an old injury.

"We are too few," Andron objected. "You were told to wait at least two generations until our numbers increased. It's only been fifteen cycles."

"He may have a point." As the oldest, Demtrie should be listened to. "In case none of the rest of you have noticed, our birth rates are lower than normal."

"Our youth are too slow to be braided," Andron offered as a way of explanation. His amber eyes looked at each of them. His white hair had thinned so a bald patch had formed making his forehead seem higher.

"There's a lack of women," Digin corrected, pulling at his ear as if his black hair tickled it. "Our records indicate if this pattern continues," he paused to make his point, "we might cease to be."

"Nonsense!" Andron threw back.

"The All Knowing One designed us to father sons," Demtrie cut in quietly. "Yes, occasionally there is a daughter, yet not enough."

"Perhaps," Rigon jumped into the conversation. "We should be addressing the need for wives rather than discussing a new Homefall, which the Talons are going to establish regardless of what we think." He patted his bald head in a nervous gesture Daniel recognized.

Andron glared at Daniel. "If you have already decided, why consult us?"

"Because we may have to." He took a deep breath unsure of the reception his next words would receive. "Pull from other Homefalls to have enough." He waited for the fall out. Each of their images showed their reactions. Not favorable.

"Not from mine," Andron informed him. His reaction not a surprise. "You choose to do this and you stand alone." He cut the com.

"Nor ours," Both Digin and Rigon said almost at the same time. "You take this risk and fail, we will not help." Their images faded.

Daniel crossed his arms and waited for the same from Demtrie.

The older man regarded the clan leader, a compassionate look on his face. "You've always been a risk taker, Daniel." He grinned. "Makes you stronger than most. I'll talk to our clan leader. I doubt he'll be supportive."

"I expected that." He moved to cut the com.

"Not so fast youngling." Demtrie rubbed his chin. "While my clan leader might not support you, I personally do." His shrewd dark brown eyes studied Daniel's face. "Right now, yours is the strongest clan and you're right, this is a needed step. Gives us all hope."

"How bad are the birth rates?" He braced himself for the answer.

"Worst I've seen." Demtrie gave no further details. "We already have two clans who joined together to survive for just that reason."

He knew, the V'ianths and T'ganths.

"Not sure if it will help them or not," Demtrie continued. "Myself." He chuckled. "I'd like a new challenge. Got a niece and nephew who might follow, if I ask them right."

"We'd be glad of the support."

"Jehna will be a good clan leader. Make sure you get her recognized quick as possible."

"We're not sure how long it will take to make it a success."

"Won't matter. Without that recognition she'll have a difficult time with the clan leaders, and everything will need to go through you."

By the planets, Demtrie Wayas was correct. Daniel had all he could do to run his own Homefall without having to speak for two. "I get your message."

"Figured you would." The older man grinned. "When you're ready to establish, let me know. I'll be there and hopefully with more."

"My thanks."

"The more ships a Homefall has the better their chances."

"I hate to lose the two I know are going." Plus their captains. "Both Jehna and Ryk are excellent Rovers."

"A price I'm sure you're willing to pay." Demtrie turned his head. Daniel could hear faint crying. "Sounds like our new addition has arrived. I'd better go pay my respects. I'll be waiting to hear from you."

"Keep the coms open."

Demtrie nodded and the com went dead.

With a sigh, Daniel stood and stretched, grimacing as his back muscles protested. Time to go see his wife and see what remedy she'd mix up, knowing he should have gone to her earlier. No doubt Taeia would scold him before fussing over him. He loved his life mate. Briefly his face shadowed as an old memory flashed through his mind and he had to force it away. Did no good to think about his daughter as there would be nothing he could do for her.

"Someday," he whispered as he left to find Taeia.

Chapter 5

Arkonna's space docks, while pristine looking, always seemed dirty to Jehna. Hints of dirt lingered on metal struts along with streaks of reddish black ooze. A scent of fuel and strongly spiced food reached her nose as she traversed between the bays toward Tamzin's brothel.

'Be careful,' Tanner warned, unhappy about staying behind.

'Guard my ship,' she replied. Thieves could be anywhere just waiting for a chance to steal whatever they could walk off with. Luckily, Rover ships had genetic locks and her Uncle Assar had made certain they were difficult, if not impossible to access by anyone else.

Reaching the main street covered in black and red stones, she followed the too quiet crowd headed further into the capital. From this distance Jehna could see the sparkling towers of the Arkon's palace and had to quell the desire to take back what he had stolen. Her uncle would make the move when necessary and she had to respect his decision.

She pushed around a noble's party, ignoring the glare the over-dressed man gave her. He hated the Rovers, she could feel it rolling off him like water over rocks. Her eyes watched him pass, his red spider silk robes flashing. On his head rested a twisted gold diadem, with matching stones.

Putting his attitude behind her, she slipped between tightly compacted buildings, the path barely large enough for one person to pass. The passage reeked of waste and littered with debris. Her knuckles found the door she sought and knocked once, paused, then twice more.

Sliding open, it allowed her entrance. Jehna stepped into the compact room, the walls lined with benches covered with soft cushions. In the back stood two doors, each covered with heavy fabric, one blue the other brown.

From behind the brown one Tamzin entered. She looked ungraceful in her tan robe glittering with intricate gold designs. Her large feline head poked out, her white head covered with mismatched black stripes.

"Hello, Tamzin," Jehna greeted.

"Ah, Captain Talon," the Charon female growled. Luckily a greeting and not a challenge. "You have business?"

"Not for anyone upstairs." The second level conducted the brothel's business while the lower housed Tamsin's personal quarters, the kitchens and sleeping mats for anyone who worked in the household.

Tamzin flexed her claws, a habit she had when a new venture presented itself. "Let us have tea and discuss."

She followed the feline behind the curtain, through a hallway and into the large kitchen. Several beings scurried about preparing food. A young boy grinned at her, turning his face quickly away. Nearby a woman, who had to be his mother, motioned him to join her. She looked about the right age and Jehna wondered if the two might be interested in the deal she had to offer.

"Tea!" Tamsin ordered as they crossed the hot room and filled with delicious smells to a smaller area behind the brothel.

Stepping into the small garden, Jehna took a deep breath, appreciating the delicate scents floating around them. "I've always liked your garden." Twitters floated down from the upper branches.

"As do I."

The boy Jehna had seen appeared with a tray holding a pot, two cups and some sort of dark brown sweets. He placed it on the rock table and hurried back inside.

"Not seen him before." Jehna took a seat on a stump with a blue cushion.

"Only been here a few days," Tamzin explained. "Father died with many debts and collectors wanted to sell them both."

Her gut tightened. One of the many little-known dirty secrets allowed under law. A family could be sold and separated to settle debts.

"I settled." Tamzin poured green liquid into both cups.

"So they owe you." She took the cup and sipped. A pleasant mint flower taste teased her tongue.

"Why do they interest you?" Tamzin had always proved to be a shrewd businesswoman.

"That's why I came to talk with you." She took another drink. "We want to start a new Homefall and I'm here to trade."

"Always trade with Rovers." Tamzin sounded more amused than angry.

"The mother and her child look like they might want a new start."

The Charon lowered her mug and stared at Jehna. "How many do you seek?"

"As many as I can fit in my hold. At least twenty-one human women or more if they'll come and their children are welcome."

"Ahhh." Tamsin paced back and forth. Always amazed Jehna how graceful the large feline could be considering she stood on her hind legs, her tail carefully hidden. "Why?"

She trusted the other well enough to tell her the truth. "I'm buying property for a new Homefall."

"You seek brides for who?"

"Local rancher who currently owns the land."

"Risky." Tamzin came close, her voice dropping. "Nobles whispering."

"Aren't they always?" She understood that about court theatrics.

"Always," she agreed. "I will listen." Tamzin took a few steps away, pushing her nose into a large purple flower. "Come back in three days. I know of many who do not wish to stay."

"Thank you." She finished her tea and rose to her feet. "What do you want in return?"

Tamzin's tail jerked from side to side, pulling her robes. "When the Messengers come, I wish to hear what they have to say."

The Messengers? Jehna blinked. Her clan had been waiting for many cycles, since long before the plague which had nearly destroyed them, for the All Knowing One to keep His promise. "I know nothing of the Messengers."

"They come soon." Large yellow brown eyes gazed at her. "When they do, you will share their words."

"When the Messengers come," Jehna promised, "I or a member of my clan, will share their message."

Satisfied, the feline lightly placed a paw on Jehna's shoulder. "They come soon."

~ * ~

Night had fallen when Jehna left Tamzin's. Voices drifted on the air and the rank smells seemed to have decreased. She followed the stone road back to the port, keeping a watchful eye. Her instincts told her another followed, yet when she glanced behind, no one seemed to be stalking her.

The door slid open when she touched her finger to the lock. Stepping inside, she saw a shadow dart away. Jehna had been right. She had been followed.

'I can deal with,' Dannon told her, lifting his black head to stare at her.

Her fingers rested on his silky fur. 'No need. If that one brings trouble, I will soon know.'

'I guard door anyway.' He circled once before settling down to bathe himself.

'As you wish,' she answered, pretty certain his diligence was not needed.

Crystal waited for her in their quarters. From their thoughts, Tanner and Hawk hunted below. She stretched her unease growing.

After being here many times, Jehna had never felt in danger. Tonight, it seemed to hover everywhere.

'Bad place,' Tanner growled.

'Always is,' she returned.

'I could scout.'

'No.' She knew more than one kind of hunter lurked around the port searching for profit. Tanner would bring a high price on the black market the Arkon allowed and ignored, despite having a law against the practice.

Three days. Tamzin asked for three days to gather what Jehna asked for. What the Charon wanted in return seemed unusual. While they'd been promised, the Messengers had yet to appear. Still, a niggling doubt tickled. Maybe the brothel owner knew something Jehna did not or had heard a rumor.

Uneasy, she made herself tea and sat down on the blue couch with her book. Crystal stretched out beside her, her purr filling the room. Normally the sound calmed her, but not this time.

~ * ~

Dannon's grumbling woke her. Jehna groaned, wanting to shut out his thoughts. A scratching on the outside hatch had interrupted his nap. He hissed, 'Make it stop.'

'I'm coming.' She crawled out of bed, Crystal briefly raising her head, before closing her eyes and going back to sleep. "I envy you," she told the Felcat as she tossed on her clothes.

Making her way to the hatch, she heard the scratching as she approached. Dannon and Tanner growled as they guarded the door, both crouched to pounce on whoever stood outside.

She activated a new device her uncle recently installed, allowing her to see the person outside without them being aware. Just outside stood a hooded figure who continually glanced around as if afraid to be observed, wearing a rich fabric only worn by nobles or the Arkon's family.

"What in the Borders?" Jehna muttered as she opened the hatch. Two clear blue eyes stared up at her. "Tis a bit late for business."

"Forgive me, Captain." The woman made no move to come inside. She nervously shifted from side to side. Perhaps from the surroundings or the fact Tanner had forced his long nose out and sniffed their visitor. "My lady bids you come."

"And who is your lady?"

Her voice dropped. "She who will one day inherit the throne."

Jehna started. Never had a Rover been summoned in such a manner. "I thought such meetings were forbidden."

The other snorted. "My lady does not follow the dictates of court. She wishes to speak with you."

While it had not been said, Jehna knew her immediate presence would be required. 'Guard the ship,' she told her companions.

Tanner darted out blocking her exit. 'Not alone.'

'Tanner,' she began.

'Not alone,' he repeated.

'Fine.' When he acted like this, it would do no good to argue. 'Dannon, you and Hawk watch the ship.' She heard the leopard's agreement and Hawk complaining about his hunt being ruined.

"You need to leave the beast here," the hooded figure told her.

"He won't stay behind."

"My lady will not approve."

"I think your lady will understand." She sealed the hatch, turning her expectant gaze upon the other woman, waiting for her to lead.

With a shake of her head, the woman headed between two ships constantly glancing behind her.

'No one follow,' Tanner informed her.

'Good.' She raised her voice slightly to be heard over the

clanking and hissing filling the night air. "What is your name?"

"I am Arda." The woman hurried out of the port and through the narrow streets, others moving out of her way as if they instinctively knew to do so.

Jehna hurried behind her, Tanner loping at her side.

Since Aris had no moons, most establishments, many open through the dark night, had lights above or around the doorways. The fixtures gave some illumination to the colorful street which had lost its dark pattern and glittered before her in hues of silver and blue.

Instead of heading for the front gate, as Jehna expected, her guide darted around the side and touched her hand to part of the high glossy fence surrounding the palace. An opening appeared and Jehna followed the woman through a dimly lit passage, the entrance closing automatically behind them, making her feel trapped.

The sleek floors inside shone and the walls gleamed. They took many twists and turns. Tanner growled not liking to be confined.

"I told you that you should have left the beast."

Jehna placed a hand on the wolf's head. He'd closed his mind although she could feel Tanner's unease. "He would not have stayed behind."

Arda shook her head and opened yet another panel taking them into an interior garden. Intoxicating sweetness filled her nose. Bright blooms of blue, purple, yellow, red and other shades Jehna had never seen before surrounded her, reminding her of the gardens her mother had kept on Sharmain. Tall trees loomed overhead, some with vines brushing the mossy gray ground.

They reached an ornate door with designs dancing across its surface. Jehna recognized some, yet not others. The mix was intriguing and she wished she had more time to examine them.

"We must hurry," Arda urged as the doors swung open and she moved inside, turning briefly to motion Jehna to follow.

She led Jehna to a large room which obviously was used as an audience chamber. A single round blue cushion sat in the center, with circles radiating out from it. From what little she knew of court life, the most trusted or privileged sat closest with others further away depending on their rank or court favor.

"Wait here." Her guide glided toward an arched entrance at the end of the large room.

'Not like wait,' Tanner told her, his eyes looking up at her.

'No choice.' She glanced around, noting the simple bluish green walls and the white stone they stood upon. Above the vaulted ceiling with clear windows to reveal the dark beauty of space and the many stars populating it. No doubt during the day the sky gave the impression of a vast room.

'Coming.' Tanner turned his huge head toward the lone figure approaching them.

Her instincts automatically summed up the woman who approached them. She moved gracefully, her long green gown loose and flowing across the floor. Her brownish blonde hair had been piled into a braided fashion and a twisted crown of silver with off white stones rested on the top of her head. Stunning pale green eyes, a trait only the Wise Women carried, met hers.

"Your Grace," Jehna greeted, inclining her head, knowing the other woman's identity from Arda's hint.

"Captain Talon," the Princess Royal answered, her voice musical.

"I came as you asked."

"And I thank you for that." She turned her attention to the wolf. "Who is this?"

"One of my companions, Tanner."

"You honor me." Her fingers lightly caressed Tanner's head. He tipped his head to the side as if trying to decide how to respond.

"How may I be of service?" Jehna asked, wondering why she'd been summoned.

"I would ask a favor of you." Her fingers produced a long golden tube from somewhere inside her gown. "Please deliver this to she who is Arvona."

Chapter 6

Three days passed and Jehna returned to Tamzin's brothel. The message from Her Grace had been secured in the vault hidden in her quarters. Crystal had expressed an interest in the tube daring to sniff it. Once the Felcat took a whiff, she backed away and refused to go near it again.

The Charon feline met her once again in her private garden, hot tea and delicate flower biscuits waiting. Jehna enjoyed both, not pushing for the results of the transaction they'd agreed upon. Once they both had eaten and finished their tea, Tamzin extended her claws and reached to scratch the riddled bark of the only tree. From what she saw, it had been used many times.

When Tamzin finished, she faced Jehna. "I have what you seek and more than I expected."

"That's a good outcome."

"Perhaps." She snatched a fleb out of the air. The tiny flying creatures pollinated flowers. Opening her paw, she released it. "How are you to feed and provide for them?"

"Uncle Daniel proved generous with supplies."

"Ah, he thought it a good trade." Her tail flicked once.

"He did."

"I will bring them to your ship just as the sun sets."

"Agreed." Jehna stood. "How many?"

"Five women with children including the woman and her son who worked for me."

Jehna's eyes narrowed. "And?" Hoping the Charon female had been more successful than the few she said.

"And." Tamzin's tongue lashed out and licked her paw. "Word of your need had passed to those who wish a new beginning. I found a good strong thirty from among the near hundred who wanted to come."

"A hundred?" The Rover captain had no idea there might be so many.

"As I said, there are many who wish a new life. They know I help to provide it. Perhaps," Her claw tapped the stone table. "You may strike a deal with others."

"I make no promises." If the other ranchers on Saris wanted brides, she might set up several lucrative trades.

"I ask for none." She chuffed. "You are good Rover. Make fair trades."

"My thanks." She stood. "I will await delivery."

~ * ~

True to her word as she always was, Tamzin delivered the future brides to *The Lady* as the sun sent orange, purple and faint green rays through the thin clouds. Jehna examined the group with interest noting the varied ages of the women. What they had in common seemed to be tired faces and some even held an expression of hope.

The small group of mothers hung together. Four had one child while the last had two, a girl and a boy. The youngster who had seen her before gave a shy wave. She smiled back.

"Welcome aboard," she greeted. "I'm Captain Jehna Talon. I have an empty hold with a cook unit and other amenities for your comfort." Jehna stepped aside. "If you'll follow Tanner he'll show you the way."

No one moved. Tanner wagged his tail trying to look friendly. He glanced up at her before going inside, looking over his shoulder as if to beseech the women and children to follow.

The boy from Tamzin's squared his shoulders and walked up the ramp. He stopped at the top. "We have a chance for a new beginnin'. You gonna squander it?"

His mother followed him. As if the pair broke a piked dam, the others followed most keeping their eyes on the ground as if afraid their chance for escape would disappear.

Jehna watched them and turned to Tamzin. "It's that bad?"

"Arkon not a bad ruler." Her long-striped tail swept side to side. "I hear his advisors were ill picked."

"What do you say?"

"Not part of the court. Only repeat what I have heard."

Jehna grinned slightly. "No doubt you hear much."

The Charon hissed slightly. "Always hear much."

~ * ~

Once again in space, Jehna went below to check on her passengers. She couldn't think of them as cargo as no doubt the slavers, who wandered the star lanes seeking able bodies for profitable customers, would. Instead, the women and children were settlers seeking a new beginning.

When she arrived, what she discovered made her happy. The new settlers had made beds for themselves all through the hold, making good use of the thick fluffs for sleeping and the blankets provided for their comfort. A few hung for privacy, while others preferred a more open sharing of the space.

"Hi, Captain," the boy from Tamzin's greeted.

"Hi." Kneeling down so she could be eye to eye with the child she asked. "What is your name?"

"Roury," he answered. "My mother is Denebie." The boy smiled proudly. "She's the best cook."

"Then I would say we are fortunate to have her."

He nodded and ran off to join the other children who played a game chasing one another.

"He's a good boy," his mother said, brushing her thick black hair out of her face. Guessing, Jehna thought the woman was perhaps thirty cycles. "I want to thank you for this chance to live a better life."

"You're welcome." She glanced around. Every eye watched them. "You do understand I'm taking you into the Tashuti Nebula to be wives for ranchers and their hands."

"So it was explained." Denebie glanced at the others. "What do you know of these men?"

"Not much. I know the owner I traded with is an honest good man. I suspect he would only hire those like him."

"But you do not know."

"I don't." No need to lie to them.

Denebie nodded, smoothing the simple faded orange dress. "Life is about risk. This is one I took for me and my son."

She hoped the others felt the same way. "I'm glad you were brave enough to do so."

"I never thought myself brave." Pale brown eyes met her green ones briefly as Denebie's gaze shifted to the metal floor.

"The past is the past. You need to lift your eyes to the future and what it might bring." Her mother had said those words to her. In the time since her death Jehna had learned their truth.

"You are wise." Denebie lifted her head.

"I had a good teacher."

~ * ~

Navigating the nebula, Jehna set an orbit around Saris while she examined the valley she wanted from above. Surrounded by mountains with one or perhaps two trails in or out, it would work perfect for easy access to the sky, a necessity for a Rover Homefall.

In the mountains she could see ancient ruins and grinned. The Dragons would pay any price to dig for treasure. While some ancient legends said the huge reptiles hoarded precious jewels or coins, the Marllonians sought knowledge, which they willingly shared with the Rovers. Her people put the technology and other secrets they'd learned to good use, establishing homes in areas thought unsuitable for settlement.

A deal with the scholars would prove lucrative for the new household and she began to plan how best to use her advantage. First though, she needed to land and introduce the future wives to their new home. No doubt Harrison Talbot awaited their delivery and the final settling of their trade.

She wondered with the extra women if she could negotiate for either rights to the ruins or the mountains themselves. Might be worth exploring the option.

"Weird control room."

"You should be below in the hold, Roury." A faint mustiness followed the boy's movements.

He shrugged, walking around the control orb with open interest. "How does this work?"

"Most Rovers are telepathic. We talk to our ships and tell them what to do."

His pale brown eyes widened. "Really?"

"Really."

"Soldiers use controls in their ships. Puters make calculations. I heard sometimes they get lost."

"That's unfortunate." She felt for the men the Arkon may have lost and felt pain for their families.

"They get compensated, so I hear." His fingers reached for the orb, before he pulled them back. "Guess I shouldn't touch."

Her eyes danced. "Not unless you want to crash," she teased.

Roury looked stricken. "That would be awfully bad."

"It would yes." Her fingers glided over the orb. "I promise I won't let that happen."

"Promise?"

"I just did."

The door slid open and the boy backed up, brushing the wall. Jehna smiled as Dannon silently entered completely ignoring Roury. The leopard's tail tip twitched slightly and he opened his mouth tasting the scents.

'Boy stinks.'

'We have to be easy on the water with this many on board.'

'Still stink.' Dannon stretched out on the floor making his body as long as possible. Rolling on his side, he turned his back on the two humans.

"Is it dangerous?" Roury asked quietly, as if afraid of the big cat.

"Not really." A partial truth and Jehna knew that.

"How'd he come to join you?"

"That's a very long story."

"Mother says that when she doesn't want to answer my question."

"Let's just say that Dannon, Tanner and Hawk all stay with me because they want to."

"What about the little cat?"

"Crystal?"

He nodded, rubbing his snub nose.

"She's a Felcat. Do you know what that is?"

"Naw," he replied, shaking his head.

"They're a very old species who have lived on many planets."

"How come?"

"They like to watch history as it happens. They remember and share it with other Felcats."

"Not with anyone else?"

"Rarely."

"Kind of selfish."

"Maybe." She couldn't disagree with his observations. Crystal rarely talked with Jehna.

"Huh." Roury edged around Dannon and headed for the door. "Gotta go. Mother's cooking."

"Enjoy your meal. Let everyone know we'll be landing soon."

"Sure thing."

Chapter 7

Harrison watched as the round mottled colored ship landed. Reminded him of a contaminated pond with its dark surface mixed with splotches of orange and green, although it probably blended into space making the ship difficult to see. Would come in handy should the Rovers ever need to smuggle merchandise. Not likely he reminded himself since they held the monopoly on the trade routes.

Muddy ground sucked at his boots as he made his way across the open space between the house and the barn. His hands ventured out of the bunkhouse curious about their visitor. Harrison just hoped the Rover captain brought wives as promised.

By the time he reached the Rover vessel the ramp had been extended and the Rover captain stood just outside the hatch. Captain Talon gave him a slight nod and a smile as she waited.

"Good to see you again," Harrison greeted, stopping not far away.

"And you," she returned. Her green eyes took in the other men huddled together not far away. "Did you tell them about our agreement?"

"Had to." He'd had some problems with a few wanting to leave before the unseasonal heavy winter storms began blocking the main roads between the other ranches and the one small town almost everyone gathered at when weather permitted. It housed a saloon with a brothel upstairs, a general store and a few other shops.

"I see." To her credit, Captain Talon didn't ask any further questions.

"Any luck?" He couldn't keep the hopeful tone out of his voice.

"More than enough."

Her answer took a metra to register. He'd figured she'd find maybe a handful. Harrison's expression must have given him away for she said, "I told you there are those who would want a fresh start." She glanced behind her as the wolf sat his huge body at the entrance. "You just need to know who to ask."

Now that made sense. From what he'd heard, Rovers had contacts on almost every world or at the very least, those who would be willing to help them. He wondered what kind of trade she'd made to get assistance to locate brides for his men.

"They're currently in the hold waiting. There's about thirty and a few who brought their children." She waited for his response.

"That's more than I asked for."

"Better to have more than needed than not enough."

"She's right." Harrison turned as Molly toddled over to join him. She wore brown gingham, her heavy boots peeking out from under her skirt. "You gave each of your hands a plot of land to call their own in the event they wanted to settle. I reckon with the prospect of a bride, they'll be wanting to do just that."

"No doubt," he agreed with his housekeeper and cook. "We've managed to convert one of the storage sheds into a dormitory for the women. Should be warm and comfortable while they're courted."

"Good to hear you planned well."

He chuckled. "I had very willing help."

~ * ~

As night dropped onto the ranch Jehna managed to get the women and children unloaded and into their new home. She let them keep the blankets, fluffs, and anything else they might need. Harrison Talbot's men had done a good job setting up a basic and usable space along with a fireplace for warmth and a cook stove.

A roast sat on the stove top cooking while a few women sliced vegetables for their dinner. Rich meat smells and spices filled the room.

The men had aided the group across the ground before getting shy and disappearing back into their bunkhouse. She suspected it might take a few days before the two groups warmed up to each other.

She turned to leave to finish the final arrangements for the land and to assure Harrison she hadn't forgotten his personal favor. Jehna would take care of that when she returned.

Denebie caught her before she reached the door. "A moment, Captain."

Jehna stepped to the side curious what Denebie wanted.

"I hear you're buying land to set up a new Rover household."

She nodded. "We'll sign the final contract tonight and transfer the property." Step one of her plan completed. The next would be finding those willing to settle it with her.

"When you do," she glanced around and lowered her voice. "My son and I would like to join you. His father," she started, swallowed and continued. "He was a Rover."

"Which clan?" She couldn't imagine any of her cousins leaving behind a child. They would have brought Denebie to the Homefall before her son was born.

"Jovan," she replied, looking down at her work-roughened hands. "Didn't know I was with child."

"I'll need a sample to confirm."

Denebie reached into her pocket and withdrew a small container, placing it carefully in her extended hand. "From his birthing."

"I'll have it tested."

"It's Roury's right." His mother seemed to think she needed to defend her decision.

"I understand," she reassured the other woman. "I'll speak to Harrison about it. He has the right to know."

She nodded. "Thank you." Denebie darted away as if she feared staying longer would change the outcome.

Jehna tucked the sample into an inner pocket in her cloak and stepped out into the crisp air. Steam rose from the ground and her boots made a crackling sound as she walked over the rapidly freezing ground. She knocked lightly and Molly opened the door, her face split into a huge grin. "Welcome!"

"Thank you." She stepped inside welcoming the warmth. After hanging her cloak Molly led her to a small office where Harrison sat, the contract in front of him. "Before you sign that, I just found out about a situation we need to discuss."

His chair creaked as he sat back waiting. Quickly she explained what Denebie had requested.

"Won't be an issue, Captain. I asked for twenty brides, you brought more."

She heard the scratching as he signed the contract. Jehna did as well, making a scan for her records. Once back on board her ship, she'd send a copy to Uncle Daniel.

"You don't mind if Denebie and her son stay here while I verify?"

"Not at all." He got up and poured some hot liquid into a cup which sat on a sideboard next to the wall. "Would you like some?"

"Thank you, no. I need to get back to my ship, record our agreement, and flyover in the morning." She watched him briefly. "When I come back, I'll have your cats and possibly a dog or two." Jehna wanted him to know she hadn't forgotten his personal favor he'd asked.

"Thank you for remembering." He paused before adding, "Before I forget I broadened the border of the property I sold you. You'll own most of the mountain territory all the way to the Ghost Sea. You'll see that in the map I added."

The ruins were located there. Jehna could not have planned this better. "I appreciate your generosity."

"Not as generous as it sounds." He sat back down. "Most of that land is useless for much of anything to do with the ranch."

"Not to worry, I can make use of the land."

He laughed. "Why does that not surprise me?"

~ * ~

Morning brought drizzling snow making Jehna glad she wouldn't have to go outside. She said her goodbyes last night and looked forward to taking a closer look at the land she now owned. Not that she'd go exploring. She wanted Cousin Ryk there when she did since she valued his opinion and he would probably notice any repairs which might need to be done before they took up residence.

Airborne *The Lady* skimmed over the mountains and hovered above the valley. The images appeared above the orb giving her more details than what she'd seen both from a distance or in space.

They'd have plenty of water, open land and a possible home as she'd observed before. Since they'd have shelter it meant they wouldn't need to live aboard their ships while they built a Homefall dwelling. The building sitting there had a high rock wall, a wide wooden gate, which even she could see would need repair. One side lay at an angle.

A tall five-sided tower faced the open fields and she smiled. They'd have a perfect place for a com tower. Radiating out from there other stone dwellings sat, plus what might be inner gardens. Once the snow melted she'd be able to take a closer look.

Who had originally built the structure might stay a mystery unless one of the dragons had seen another similar. Odd to think another race might have once roamed this area of space and left behind signs of their civilization. Wouldn't be the first time ruins had been found.

'Not us,' Tanner sleepily said. 'We didn't like traveling among the stars.'

'Didn't say it was,' she replied, amused by the wolf's comment.

He fell silent. Dannon had decided to take a nap or so he'd informed her earlier. Hawk had discovered a large rodent and he'd shut out his thoughts as he shredded and ate it. Crystal had been curled up on the couch and no doubt would stay there for most of the flight back to Ronia.

"Time to go home," she murmured, setting the course and navigating the nebula. Jehna noticed an Arkon vessel, shaped like one of Hawk's wings, just outside the gaseous border. With a shrug she figured they were just patrolling, although they normally didn't roam far from the Five Systems. The Borders they normally left alone. She'd mention their presence to Uncle Daniel and see if he had any idea why they might be there.

She set her course home and slipped through space, happy the deal had been completed and they had the land for a new Homefall. Now what she needed were Rovers to fill it.

Chapter 8

"What do you think, Ryk?" Jehna asked as a cold wind wrapped around the stone corner and pulled at her cloak.

"Sturdier than I would have thought," he returned, his gray eyes taking in the building she hoped would prove sturdy enough to use as their new home. "Built to withstand the elements." He patted the neatly packed stone of the five-sided tower. "Been inside yet?"

"One of Uncle Daniel's lessons…"

"…Never enter an ancient structure alone," he finished, a grin on his wide face. "Shall we take a look?"

"Might as well."

Together they entered the intricately carved door leading to the interior. Ryk pulled a glow globe out of his black murhide cloak. How he'd managed to trade for one of the rarest items in the Borders Jehna had no idea. Maybe one day he'd tell the story behind it.

The globe's light danced off sparkles on the interior walls. She exchanged a look with her cousin as they slowly advanced into the structure, the walls taking unexpected twists.

"Be hard to break in here." Ryk took a final turn leading into the main interior. "Feels almost like a maze."

"Except no maze has that." She pointed at the large fireplace made from what she guessed to be smooth river rocks and a silent pond with what looked like a waterfall. A few plants shivered as if sensing them.

"Interesting design." He moved closer to the fireplace, the light showing it went well up the wall disappearing into a high ceiling they could barely see.

"I wonder what is this way?" She waited for Ryk to join her.

"Let's go find out."

Around another wall, they found what had to be a cooking area. Long flat surfaces lined one wall, with some sort of cook stove with a sink on the farthest and behind them, Jehna gasped, stood a huge cupboard.

"I say you chose well, Cousin." Ryk ran his hand across the cupboard. "This is handmade."

"And whoever built this place just walked away and left it."

"Fortunate for us." He gave her an odd look. "You have no sense about this place?"

"None. Feels empty. Abandoned."

"All the better." He moved out into the connecting hall and followed it.

"Surely you don't believe in spirits." She hadn't since she'd been very young.

"I believe there is more in the universe than we can explain." He stopped. "Found a way up."

Broad stairs had been carved into one huge glittering boulder and led up.

"I wonder how they got this here?"

"One of the many mysteries I'm sure we'll discover." He headed up and she followed.

At the top Ryk pushed open a door and they entered a huge room. Windows opened out onto the snowy field on several sides and from what she could see a small living area.

"I had a feeling this would be perfect for a com room." Jehna stood looking out over the open field. The sun briefly flickered through the thick clouds revealing sleek wavy patterns in the snow. "Wonder what made those?"

Her cousin came to stand beside her. "Hard to say without a closer look." The globe had dimmed while he held it in his hand. "If the rest of the buildings are in similar shape, we can move in whenever we wish."

"Depending on how many we convince to start this household with us." Jehna couldn't keep the bitterness out of her voice.

"We're the first new Homefall in generations." Lightly he touched her arm. "Have faith in the All Knowing One, Jehna."

"I do." She'd been raised to believe in both the All Knowing One and the Great Mother. A fact Altair had reminded her of when the healer and her daughter Arissa arrived on Ronia. Not all the Wise Women had changed their beliefs.

"There will be you and I," Ryk began, "Plus the Wise Woman and her child, and my daughter Tuleh."

"Two ships, Ryk." She shook her head. "Not enough to keep a Homefall supplied."

"It'll be enough for a small one."

"Well, we may have another two occupants. I'm waiting for Aunt Taeia to finish the sequencing." She'd also delivered her message from the Princess Royal. The Arvona had not seemed surprised to receive the missive.

"The possible Rover boy and his mother."

"I worked it out with Harrison. Good thing I brought more potential wives than what he needed."

"Importing wives may be an excellent way to trade for supplies, not to mention gain allies among the ranchers," Ryk slyly suggested.

"And we may need them." Harrison had hinted the winters could be brutal. "We have at least one."

"It's a good beginning. I think we should get below and explore while we have light. Come night we both should be back aboard our ships."

"Agreed." She glanced around the potential com tower before taking the stairs back to the main level.

After exploring the main structures close to the tower, one of which connected to the five-pointed sides, they headed back to where they'd left their ships. *The Lady* hovered a few metras off the frozen ground, the *Starrite* not far away.

"Before we wait out the night, I'd like to see what made those patterns in the snow." Ryk took off in the direction they'd seen from above. Jehna hurried after him.

Blazed through the white intricate patterns danced and crisscrossed oddly rippled and varying in size. Ryk knelt down, pulling a bright blue object from one of the paths. "This is a scale."

Her memory jumped back to the odd dragon she and Harrison had seen. The large reptile had proved harmless after they'd returned its young. "Dragon."

"Dragon?" He rose.

"The Ghost Mountains have native dragons. I saw one."

He pointed to the designs. "I'd say there are quite a few."

Examining the evidence she had to agree. "I wonder if they'll come back."

"Guess we'll find out."

~ * ~

Morning brought another surprise. A third ship had landed while Jehna slept. She recognized the purple ship with yellow zags as belonging to the Wayas clan. Vaguely she remembered Uncle Daniel sharing what the clan leaders thought and about some possible recruits for the new Homefall.

"We've got company," Ryk observed as he joined her.

Tanner bounded out and stopped, his head up and alert, his nose testing the air. He dashed across the snow as the hatch opened and the ramp descended from the Wayas ship. Three figures in family colors exited, each wearing a heavy sektile coat. Behind them came two others and Jehna immediately recognized Altair and Arissa.

"Must have stopped on Ronia," Jehna observed.

"Best we greet them."

"Where's your daughter?"

"Rearranging the main hold. She anticipates some much-needed trade and has decided we'll need the room."

"Smart like her father."

He nodded although a strange sad look crossed his face.

An older man stood waiting for them. Jehna greeted him with a smile. "I'm Jehna Talon."

"Demtrie Wayas," he returned, his dark hair smattered with white lifting slightly as a breeze rifled through it. He wore no braid. "My blood niece and nephew; Holly and Forrest."

The red headed pair nodded. Both had startling blue eyes and a smattering of freckles across the bridge of their noses. With a start, Jehna realized they were twins. Very rarely did a Rover give birth to two babies at once, let alone both a girl and a boy.

"Welcome," she greeted. "My cousin Ryk Sargol. What brings you here?"

Demtrie chuckled. "Seems your uncle neglected to tell you we were coming to join you."

"You're interested in being part of a new Homefall?" She wanted to make certain.

"Just like the healer and her apprentice." He pointed at his two passengers. "Picked them up and brought them along."

Ryk frowned. "We hadn't reported back whether we could move into our new Homefall or not."

"Well, thing about being a clan leader, sometimes you slip through space without much minding where you end up."

"Fortunate for us the buildings are solid." Her cousin pointed at the fortress. "Needs some work."

"Wouldn't be a good Homefall if it didn't," Demtrie replied good naturedly.

~ * ~

As the sun set over the Ghost Mountains, casting long shadows over the peaks, Jehna stood at her ship's hatch, watching the Wise Woman Altair Dawne approach. She moved gracefully in her gray cloak as if her feet never touched the ramp. Pausing before the Rover Captain, she waited.

"My Uncle told me you were coming," Jehna said. They hadn't had much time to talk after they'd first met.

"It was time for us to leave and seek a new home." Her seafoam eyes glided to the young girl who had come with her. Arissa couldn't have been more than nine or perhaps ten cycles. The young girl held her hand out to Tanner who sniffed her and turned his head toward Jehna.

'Smell right,' he informed her.

"Why my Homefall?" The Captain crossed her arms over her chest not sure if the healer would answer or not.

"Felt right for us both."

Same as it had to her when Uncle Daniel had proposed the idea and when she'd first seen the valley. The healer's answer, though simple, made perfect sense.

"Your Aunt sent this." Altair handed Jehna a small round disk. "She only told me it held some genetic material you had asked about."

"Thank you."

"She is Arvona."

Arvona to the Wise Women and High Priestess to the Great Mother who most believed in.

"I believe you follow the teachings of the All Knowing One." Altair's tone dared her to deny it.

"I respect the beliefs of my mother," she answered. "But I chose my path before I came of age."

"As is your right." Altair glanced at her daughter again. "I trust we are welcome here."

Jehna frowned. "Of course. Why would you not be?"

"You too are a healer."

Ah, now she understood. "My responsibilities as Clan Leader will prevent me from being the Homefall's Wise Woman. That will be your privilege."

A slight smile touched her thin lips. "Thank you for clarifying."

Jehna nodded and watched the Wise Woman take her child's hand. They both returned to the *Chaser* and disappeared inside. The Wayas additions had gone with Ryk to explore a bit more and she suspected Demtrie would come back with some ideas on how to upgrade the building so they could move in as soon as possible.

Holding the disc tightly in her hand, she went back into her ship. The test would dictate whether or not she added two more members to her household. Luckily, Harrison Talbot had agreed to the slight change in their trade, much to her relief.

Once in her quarters she examined the results. They confirmed Denebie's claims her son was of Rover blood, specifically the Jovans. She wondered if her uncle had notified their clan leader and what the outcome had been. Would he demand the boy and his mother move to their Homefall? Or would he accept she wanted to be part of Jehna's?

She'd have to wait and see. Negotiating took time and it would depend on the price set. Maybe her uncle would meet it or he might shift the responsibility to her. Only, he couldn't do that until Jehna had been recognized as the clan leader of the Saris Homefall.

'Ryk come,' Tanner informed her.

'I'll be right there.' Pushing aside her concerns until a decision was made she left her quarters and met her cousin at the hatch.

He tugged his cloak tighter and pointed behind him with a grin. "Guess who just joined us?"

Floating just above the ground floated another ship, with Talon colors, and she shook her head recognizing it as the *Ravid*, belonging to her cousin Adrian Colon. Jehna had not been expecting him.

"Go find out why he's here?" Ryk asked, watching her closely.

"Why not?" Jehna grabbed her cloak, which she kept near the hatch and threw it around her shoulders.

Together they approached the new arrival as the ramp extended and the hatch opened. Adrian smiled and waved, bouncing down to greet them. "Hi!"

"Wasn't expecting you," Jehna said as she smiled at her younger cousin. He'd turned eighteen cycles not long ago.

He pushed his long light brown hair out of his face, his golden-brown eyes sparkling. "I went to one of the Earth colonies to trade."

Ryk frowned. "I thought the Arkon isolated them."

Adrian shrugged. "He never snoops beyond the confines of his palace."

Jehna felt a shiver crawl down her back. "We hope."

"Why the trade?" Ryk demanded.

"You know how hard it is to find just cats?" He crossed his arms across his chest. "The Earth colony had plenty and were more than willing to share. I managed to pick up six, four females two of which are carrying young." She heard faint barking. "Got a couple of dogs too."

While she hadn't forgotten her promise to Harrison, Jehna hadn't had an opportunity to fulfill it. "What's your price?"

Adrian grinned. "Deal is me and soon to be life mate, once braided, get to join your Homefall."

Secretly his wish both surprised and delighted her. "Does Uncle Daniel know?"

"He will as soon as Errl tells him."

"Errl!" Ryk stared at Adrian, his gray eyes reflecting surprise.

A huge grin on his face, he nodded. "You're about to get all the Wellers."

Jehna blinked trying to take in what Adrian shared. What that meant was five more ships for her Homefall. Errl Weller, oldest of the group, captained the *Clln*. His younger brother Mark, the *Pride* and his braided life mate Gem Morran the *Cresent*. The couple had four children. Their blood cousin, Aaron, had named his ship *Anybody's Guess* due to a running childhood joke about what he'd name his future vessel.

"You all right?" Ryk looked at her concerned.

Shaken, she nodded. "I just didn't expect this many." Hoped for yes and no doubt the All Knowing One had taken a hand. She'd remember to thank Him later. "We have the room."

"Demtrie says not many repairs are needed," Ryk informed her. "Most we can move right into." He glanced at Adrian. "Plenty of room to expand."

"Errl and the rest of the family will be here in a day or two." Adrian had spent time apprenticing aboard the *Clln* and considered himself a Weller. Jehna and the rest of the clan did as well.

"We'll be ready," Jehna promised.

Chapter 9

"We're going to need horses." Ryk told Jehna the next day as they looked over the rough stone stable and corral.

Jehna nodded. Having horses would make riding to the ranches much easier and not cost expensive fuel.

"Still going to walk to the Triple D ranch?"

She rubbed her forehead, overwhelmed with the number of decisions she needed to make. Granted Jehna had been trained to lead, but following her uncle around to learn had been one thing. Being responsible for everyone's welfare quite another.

"Ideas on trade?" her cousin pushed.

"Ryk, why don't you go with me and meet Harrison Talbot." Her uncle had always delegated and she needed to learn from his example. "Demtrie can continue to check the buildings and submit a list of needed repairs when we get back."

He nodded, a slight smile touching his lips.

"Maybe by tomorrow at the latest, we can start moving into our new quarters." That prospect made her happy. The Wellers hadn't arrived yet, so they wouldn't need to accommodate them and Adrian would be leaving at nightfall to collect his bride. She suspected after they were braided, the entire group would return. No way would the Wellers miss the ceremony.

Hawk sounded a warning cry and she turned to locate the russet-colored bird in the sapphire sky. He soared low; swooping over a group headed their way on horseback.

Ryk lightly touched her shoulder. "Looks like we have company."

Jehna smiled. "That's Harrison Talbot." He had others with him and she could see a young boy waving wildly. "And that's Roury and his mother."

"More Rovers." Ryk rubbed the back of his neck.

Tanner dashed out of wherever he'd been exploring and loped to escort their visitors in. His tail wagged and greeted them with excited yips.

"I have to wonder sometimes," Ryk commented. "If they even remember they're intelligent lizards."

"No idea. I've never asked." She motioned with her hand. "Let's greet our visitors."

They met the party partway. Harrison gave them a huge smile. "Thought I'd make things easier on you."

She didn't miss the other woman riding with him, who offered up a shy smile. Dark blonde hair rested on her shoulders and her pale brown eyes glanced around.

Harrison dismounted, patting his horse's neck. Roury rushed past him and threw his arms around the wolf. To his credit, Tanner gave the boy a lick, while sniffing his hair.

'Boy happy to be here.'

Jehna pretty much knew that and found no reason to argue with Tanner.

Roury's mother slid off her horse and frowned. "You shouldn't bother the wolf."

"Ah, he's okay," her son replied. "Aren't you." Roury scratched behind the wolf's ears. Tanner's eyes half closed, enjoying every moment of attention. "Where's the big cat?"

"Dannon is sleeping in *The Lady's* hold." He'd been up all night prowling around the building exploring. The leopard had come home at first light and was taking a well-deserved rest.

"Oh." He stopped scratching. Tanner whined and the boy started up again.

'Attention monger,' she accused the wolf. He made no response.

"I'm glad to see you, Harrison." She glanced at her cousin. "This is my second in command Ryk Sargol. Ryk this is Harrison Talbot."

"Good to meet you," Ryk greeted. "Will be nice to have a friendly neighbor."

Harrison chuckled. "Word got around you supplied me with potential wives. Other ranchers may come calling."

"My contact said she had more who might want to come." His news made Jehna happy. "I'd be happy to trade."

"Figured." Harrison held the horse's reins. "The personal favor?"

"Adrian brought them last night." No need to tell him where they'd been found. "I'd like to keep one of the males and one of the pregnant female cats, if you don't mind."

"Depends on how many." Harrison sounded like he would be willing to negotiate.

"Four, one male and three females, one carrying young."

He nodded, a slow smile spreading on his lips. "That's fine." Pointing to the building he added, "Looks like you might need them."

'I hunt,' Dannon grumbled. 'So does Hawk.'

'Go back to sleep,' she told the leopard. 'The cats can get into places you can't.'

Dannon huffed and blocked her. She shook her head. Returning her attention to Harrison she went on. "Got some dogs for you too."

He sighed heavily. "You have no idea how much I appreciate that. Really missed having a dog around the ranch." His eyes darted at the still mounted woman. "Good for kids too."

So, Harrison had found a possible wife. He deserved a good woman at his side.

The rancher noticed the direction of her gaze. "That's Lissa."

The woman smiled again, looking completely at ease in her slacks and heavy coat. "Thank you for bringing me here."

"You're welcome."

Jehna hoped all the brides found good husbands.

"This who is getting the cats and dogs?" Adrian panted as he trotted to join them.

"It is."

"Good. No offense," he nodded to the rancher, "but I'd like to get them off my ship so I can leave tonight."

Harrison frowned. "You're not staying."

"Not yet. Got to go collect my bride and get braided first before we come back."

She quickly introduced her cousin and Harrison to each other. "We've made a deal. I keep one of the males and one of the pregnant females."

"You get first choice," Ryk interjected.

Jehna agreed. Harrison had that right.

"What about us?" Denebie looked expectantly at Jehna.

"Ryk, will help you get settled. Adrian, if you'd show Harrison what you brought and allow him to choose."

"Sure." Adrian grinned.

"Lissa?" Harrison went to the woman. "Want to come?"

She nodded and he helped her down. Her legs wobbled slightly. Jehna had no doubt it was the first time Lissa had ridden a horse.

The warm smile the rancher gave the pretty woman tugged at Jehna's heart. One of her goals had been to find someone special for him. Looks like she may have succeeded.

~ * ~

Harrison decided to stay long enough to eat the midday meal with the Rovers as he followed Adrian to his ship. Lissa glanced around with interest as they went inside, going down a long hallway and below via some stairs. They were led to what seemed a small hold, where the cats had been secured in a large pen where the top could be opened and the dogs in another.

The dogs were on the large side, with thick tan and white coats. Their eyes bright and inquisitive as they appeared to be watching everything going on.

"They're actually mixed breeds," Adrian explained. "They are supposed to have stock guardian breeds in their lineage."

Harrison nodded. "Where'd you find them?"

The Rover shifted slightly. "Let's just say I found a good place to trade."

Why did Harrison have the impression the young man had traded somewhere no one knew about? Not that it really mattered. He'd only asked for one dog and been supplied with three.

"Here are the cats." Adrian moved to the second enclosed pen.

Brown, blue and green eyes stared at him. He noticed two smaller areas, separated from the other four cats. They smelled strongly and he understood the males were marking their territory.

"Tried to keep it clean." Adrian shrugged.

"I understand their nature." He looked over the two male cats. One was all black, with smooth fur, the other was gray, with long hair and much larger than he'd ever seen. "I'll take the black male."

His eyes looked at the females. "Which ones are pregnant?"

"Light gray female and the brown and black striped one."

"Are the other two cats male or female?"

"Female and young."

The other two blinked their eyes and started grooming their fur. One had white fur and the other brown. He decided they'd make a good addition and some colorful kittens. So would the striped female. Harrison pointed to her. "That one."

"May I have the white cat?" Lissa asked him. "I would like one in the house."

He'd picked Lissa as a possible wife because she rarely asked for anything. She helped out in the house and got along with his house-keeper. They hadn't talked about children yet, although he'd seen her expression as she watched the few children play and recognized her yearning. Her desire equaled his own.

"Sure," he agreed.

"You want to take them now?" Adrian waited patiently for his answer.

"Mind if I leave them here awhile. I need to talk some business with Jehna."

"Not a problem."

They followed Adrian out. Harrison glanced at the sky. Clouds rolled over the sky. They might get wet going home. Good thing he'd brought the long coats and dry saddle packs for the cats. The dogs could walk.

He found Jehna talking to Ryk. They both sat on the ramp from her ship. From how close they seemed to be he wondered if they were a couple. Not one to pry, he wouldn't ask.

"Made my choices," he informed the Rover captain.

"Good. Anything else you need?"

"Got a shipment of horses waiting on Valhalla."

"I can pick them up," Ryk volunteered.

"What's your price?"

"Two horses for our household."

Harrison rubbed his jaw. His shipment contained ten specially designed horses to survive the rough winters and climb the mountain trails. Given where the Rovers were settling he surmised they'd need the same. Two horses seemed steep, yet given Jehna had more than fulfilled both the wives and his personal favor, plus he suspected he might need the alliance, he decided to agree. "Done."

"Have you paid or do you need me to deliver?"

One thing he admired about the Rovers, they were all about giving full service. "Already made." The payment had cost him every saved credit he had.

Overhead thunder rolled across the sky as the clouds darkened. Harrison had hoped to stay longer, but knew he needed to get over the mountain pass before the trails got too slick. So much for staying and sharing a meal with his new neighbors.

"Lissa, grab our coats off my horse and yours, plus the packs. Forgive me for leaving quickly. We need to get going."

"Understood." Jehna motioned to Adrian.

"How soon do you want delivery?" Ryk stood, waiting for his answer.

"Brought the receipt." He pulled out a short black stick and handed it to the Rover Captain.

"My thanks."

"You're welcome anytime, Harrison." Jehna stood and glanced at Lissa who had returned with two long coats and the packs.

"Open invite to marriages, if you'd like to attend." He hoped she'd agree.

"We'd love to attend."

Rain began to fall. He tossed on his coat and grabbed the packs from Lissa. They needed to get the cats and dogs and get moving. "See you soon."

"May the All Knowing One guide your path."

He appreciated the blessing and nodded his thanks. Thunder crashed overhead and he hurried to the ship to collect the animals. The ride was going to be very wet.

Chapter 10

Jehna watched her guests depart from inside her ship as thick rain fell from the sky. The dogs dashed around the horses and the cats had been secured in watertight bags on the backs of the other two horses. She hoped they made it safely over the mountain pass and home.

Ryk turned the receipt over in his fingers. "I'll leave as soon as the storm is over."

"Good plan." The raging storm would give her a chance to determine the weather and safe flying conditions. "Hope it stops before Adrian leaves."

"He thinks he can fly through anything."

"That's what I'm afraid of." Last thing she needed was for her cousin to misjudge the storm and end up grounded with repairs.

"Don't worry, Jehna, Errl trained him well."

"He's still impulsive."

"Maybe his bride will calm his fire."

She laughed, understanding the double reference. "Shame on you."

"'Tis truth."

"Want to take a look at that?" She meant the receipt.

"Do that later and leave tomorrow."

"How did Denebie and her son settle in?"

"Found a couple of rooms just off the kitchen. She wants to be our cook."

"She's good." Jehna remembered that from the time they'd been aboard her ship.

"They didn't have much. I made sure they had mats to sleep on and blankets. We should ask Uncle Daniel if we can have anything from the stores."

"I'll ask him. Need to talk to him anyway."

"You'd better claim your cats from Adrian."

She chuckled. "He's going to want to leave as soon as he can."

Thunder rolled across the valley. Jehna pulled her cloak tighter around her. Rain didn't fall often on arid Ronia.

"I'd wait until the rain lets up. He can't leave until it does." Ryk pulled his cloak tighter.

She nodded having come to the same conclusion earlier. "I noticed a room on the upper level I might like."

"Lots of levels," he agreed. "I have to wonder what this was originally designed for."

"Hard to say." The night lit up, rapidly followed by crashing.

'Too loud,' Tanner whined. He brushed against Jehna. Her fingers touched his fur, smoothing it back on his skull.

"It's just a storm."

Ryk glanced at her and then at the wolf. "If this is an example of the weather,"

She was already ahead of him. "I'll have a talk with Harrison." He'd been on his ranch for years. No doubt he knew the patterns.

"I'm going to make a run for my ship." He pulled his hood over his head. "Need to go over the receipt and help my daughter get our ship ready."

"Two horses?" She gave her cousin a teasing smile.

"Be a start." He dashed across the muddy field, pounding up the ramp of the *Starrite*. The hatch retracted.

'Inside?'

"Yeah." Pressing the controls she retracted the ramp and closed the door. When the storm stopped she'd retrieve her cats. In the meantime, she'd call Uncle Daniel.

Leaving her cloak by the door, she climbed to the upper level. Tanner left her to return to the hold. In the control room, she called her clan leader, updating him about the arrival of the Wayas plus the healer and her daughter.

"I knew they were joining you," his image told her.

"Did you know the Wellers are as well?"

His silence gave her his answer.

"They didn't tell you." She suspected they hadn't.

He shook his head. "I'll have a word with Errl when they're here for Adrian's braiding." His gaze shifted to her. "You are coming."

"Of course." She knew the clan always gathered for important occasions. Since she was still technically a Talon and would be until she'd been confirmed as a clan leader, she'd be expected to attend.

Daniel relaxed. "Good."

"I take it the Jovans will be in attendance."

"They will." He grinned. "Should be a lively celebration."

~ * ~

Harrison stopped at the house first, helping Lissa dismount. He ushered her into the house. Molly met them at the door.

"You're soaked," she accused, helping the poor girl out of coat. "Go and take a hot bath and warm up, Lissa. I left some dry clothes in the washroom."

"Thank you." Lissa looked a bit pale and her teeth chattered. Harrison felt bad about that and watched as she headed toward the back of the house.

"Mind if I leave the cats with you, Molly?" He knelt down and opened the saddle bags. Several feline heads popped out, their noses sniffing.

"Not at all." Molly grinned watching as they reluctantly stepped on the floor. "They'll be running the place before you know it."

He laughed. "Need to tend the horses and put the dogs in the barn."

"Mercy sakes, dogs too?" Molly shook her head. "Them Rovers have been busy."

"You could say that." He went back out and got the animals into the barn, settling the horses into their stalls. The dogs shook their fur and began sniffing around the barn.

With a smile, Harrison took off the saddles and toweled the horses dry. He made sure they had water and sweet grass to eat. After he put the saddles and bridles in the tack room, he tossed warm blankets over them, talking to them in a gentle reassuring voice.

He glanced at the dogs, who were now laying near the horse stalls. The Rover said they came from stock guardian lines. It would appear they were already settling into the job.

Back in the house, he hung up his coat, his nose detecting the smell of spicy beans and cornbread. Molly always seemed to know what dish to serve.

"Lissa's out of the tub. Best you get warmed up," she called from the table. "Dinner will be ready in a few."

"Where's Lissa?"

"Guest room. Poor thing's exhausted. Gave her some tea and suggested she have a lie down." Molly put her hands on her hips. "What were you thinking, taking the girl over the Ghost Mountains?"

He shrugged. "I warned her it was a hard ride. She wanted to go anyway."

"She must really like you then." She tapped her foot. "Best you marry that gal before one of the hands snatches her up."

"Molly," he warned.

"You've been single long enough." With a huff, Molly headed back to the kitchen.

Running a hand through his hair, Harrison grabbed some clean clothes and used the washroom. He soaked in a hot tub thankful he put in a pump and a heater. Lingering so his cold limbs could warm, he pondered Molly's words.

Had he been single long enough? He couldn't be sure, but admitted to himself it would be nice to have a wife beside him at night. Been too long since he'd had a woman and he had no intention of using the ladies in town to soothe his needs.

Rising, allowing the cooler air to help dry him, he used a thick towel and dressed. He found Molly had set the table and Lissa sat opposite him. She gave him a shy smile.

"Food smells wonderful." She helped herself to some beans and cornbread.

"Molly's a great cook." He filled his bowl and took a swig of cof.

"If I eat like this all the time, I'll get fat." Her eyes darted up and her cheeks turned a dark pink.

"Working on a ranch is hard work." He tasted the beans. Nice and spicy just as he liked them.

"Molly fed the cats." She took a bite, chewed and swallowed before she spoke again. "Do you mind if I name them?"

"Except the white one, they'll be barn cats."

"Doesn't mean they and the dogs shouldn't have names." Her look dared him to argue. "You named your horses."

Harrison couldn't argue with her reasoning. "You're right." He gave her a smile.

Took a moment for her to realize she'd won. Her smile lit up her face. "Thank you."

"You're welcome."

They ate in silence, the fire popping in the background.

"You should stay here tonight in the guest room." The storm had gotten worse and he could hear the rain hitting the roof. "No need for you to get soaked going back to the dorm."

She pushed her beans around. "My stayin' will give everyone the wrong impression."

"Molly is in the house and a good chaperone."

Lissa blushed again. "I hadn't thought of that."

"I understand." He had no intention of touching the woman until they were wed. If they wed, he reminded himself. Not like he'd asked her or she'd consented.

She nodded and finished her dinner before slipping into the guest room. Harrison cleared the table taking the dishes to the kitchen. Molly sat in a chair, watching the cats, who ate food from bowls on the floor.

"One of these going to stay in the house?" she asked.

"The white one." He leaned against the sink. "Lissa's going to name them."

Molly grinned. "Good." She made shooing motions with her hands. "I'll finish clearing the table. You best get to bed."

"Night, Molly."

"Night."

He banked the fire before heading for his room. The guest room door opened and Lissa whispered, "Good night."

"Night," he returned before going to bed. Overhead the rain pounded and tired as he was, Harrison wondered if he'd be able to sleep. These type of nights he and his wife used for loving. Not something he could ask of Lissa quite yet.

Forcing himself underneath the covers, Harrison closed his eyes and knew he needed to sleep. He had chores tomorrow, rain or not.

As he dropped off he wondered how the Rovers were coping with the weather.

Chapter 11

"You leaving, Ryk?" Jehna asked her cousin the next morning as he joined her for the morning meal. Light rain fell outside and thunder rolled across the valley.

He nodded. "Tuleh has the *Starrite* ready to go and the hold adapted to load horses." Ryk shrugged. "Rain is not heavy enough to delay."

She didn't like it, yet her cousin was a seasoned Rover and she saw no cause to stop him. "Just be home in time for the braiding."

"We'll unload our cargo and come straight away."

"I'll hold you to that."

He chuckled. "I can't wait to see the bride Adrian chose."

"Healer from what I heard."

"Huh." His eyes rested on Altair and her daughter, sitting by the fireplace. "We've more than enough. Unusual for a household."

"Taeia and I were both on Ronia." Jehna reminded him, sipping her tea.

"True," he agreed. "I'd best be off." Ryk rose and headed for the main door. "Might want to decide if you want that fountain to work or not."

"I'll consider it." She watched him leave and shook her head. Ryk was definitely a good choice for her second. He could see what needed to be done.

Her gaze rested on the others sitting in the odd five-sided room. Demtrie and his cousins played a game of stars and pebbles, a favorite among the clans. Object of the games was to collect as many of both and whoever had the least, lost. Altair had several plants she was showing her daughter. She knew at one time the healer had been wed. Jehna knew better than to ask about how he died. If the wise woman wanted to share her story, she would.

Her new cook and son, she could hear in the kitchen. They chattered happily and she was glad they'd joined the household. Her companions she hadn't seen and suspected they'd gone hunting. According to Tanner, there were plenty of small animals who tasted good.

Demtrie sat down opposite her. "All well?"

She nodded. "Ryk is making a run."

"Good." His fingers tapped the tabletop. "You two work well together."

"We grew up together."

"Not my business, but are you two considering being braided?"
Jehna shook her head.

"Hmmm." He scratched his lined face no doubt pondering her answer. "Discovered there's a living area in the tower with room enough for one."

"Volunteering to man the com?" If he did, it would solve many issues of trying to figure out who would best be suited for the role.

"Sure am." He tapped his leg. "Forrest and Holly been running my ship for the past couple of cycles."

She'd noticed his limp. "You're wanting to ground."

"Been wanting to," he agreed with a tired smile. "I backed Daniel and convinced my clan chief to do the same. Took some talking."

"Thank you." Jehna needed the support.

"Whether the others see it or not, a new household is needed." He got to his feet. "Going to get myself settled and set up the com room, if that's okay with you."

"It's fine. I appreciate your willingness to help."

He chuckled. "Setting up the com no matter how badly needed, isn't a task most want."

~ * ~

The *Starrite* landed on Valhalla, which sat on the edge of space between the Borders and the Five Systems. Ryk knew the Arkon's military irregularly patrolled the area. They'd never caused any issues and he hoped that continued.

The owner, wearing only a loincloth, hobbled across the landing field, waving a hairy arm. In the other he dragged a youngster by their tail who squealed loudly. Ryk waved back trying not to cringe at the show of dominance. Not far away the baby's mother pursued, no doubt trying to figure out how to rescue her child.

His daughter stopped beside him making a face, yet kept her silence. She wore the Talon color; the black making her fair skin lighter and her red hair even more noticeable. Her mother had refused to wear them since they were unflattering.

He pushed his mind away from his dead wife. She'd died ten cycles ago, her ashes interred in the family wall. Their daughter had been five. With the clan's help he'd raised their child and apprenticed her on his ship.

Ryk glanced at his daughter realizing Tuleh was almost of age. He wondered if a Rover man had caught her eye yet and if one had, when she'd tell him.

"You've got that look," Tuleh commented. She smiled as their smelly host stopped. Her voice dropped. "I keep forgetting how hairy they are."

"You were seven your first and only visit," Ryk reminded his daughter.

"You have receipt?" the simian demanded, long fingers extended. The dirt covered child chittered unhappy at its situation.

"I'm picking up a shipment for Harrison Talbot." Ryk handed over the receipt.

"Ah, yes, ten adapted for ranch work and climbing mountains." With a motion they followed across the hard ground, the young one again being dragged by its tail. The mother still close by. Overhead lavender clouds rushed across a sky of pale mauve. Faint scents of wild grass and flowers floated in the misty air.

In a fenced pasture next to the landing field ten horses munched on yellow flowers. Their tales brushed against their hindquarters and their ears twitched. One with deep brown colors turned its head as if inspecting Ryk and Tuleh.

"They're beautiful," she breathed, climbing up the wooden fence for a better view.

Ryk noticed the differences. Stocky legs, slightly larger hooves, colors ranging from browns to shades of black.

"Talbot be pleased?" Black eyes stared at Ryk. The youngster managed to climb the fence and sit on top, its tail firmly gripped by the adult male.

"No doubt."

A high pitch sound escaped the simian's muzzle and two others similar to him darted out, one grabbing a horse so black the fur had a blue sheen to it.

"Stud. Leader. Others follow," their host explained.

"Thank you." Ryk had studied what information they had on horses when he realized they would need the animals to make the new Homefall successful.

"Tell Talbot, he has breeding rights." A look that seemed to be a frown crossed the breeder's face. "Too far out not to allow."

"Understood." Ryk took a deep breath. "I'm claiming two in payment. Is the privilege extended?"

"For Rovers?" The other looked surprised. "Not use for trade."

"Personal use."

"Granted." He pointed to two horses. One had a white patch on its brown forehead and the other a white spot on its black back. "Those two best."

Ryk had to hide his grin. Not exactly a breach of contract, but the breeder, no doubt in the future, would want a favor. "My thanks." He gave a slight bow. "Tuleh, show them where to take the horses."

"Sure thing." She jumped down and led the way to the ship.

He turned to their host who returned the receipt. "What favor would you ask?"

"Right time. I ask."

~ * ~

"We're on our way back," Ryk reported his image floating above the orb.

"Pick out a couple of good ones for us?" Jehna asked.

Her cousin chuckled. "The breeder told me which ones to take."

"In return for?" She knew the simians loved to make deals.

"To be determined."

"Should be interesting."

"That's what I thought. They want something, but aren't ready to ask."

"How are the horses doing?" Their ships weren't designed for large animals, but she knew Ryk and Tuleh made accommodations.

"Fine. How's everyone settling in?"

"Pretty well. Altair and her daughter found a chamber to fit their needs on the upper level. Forrest and Holly picked one of the smaller buildings." She laughed. "Turns out it's attached to the main building."

"Handy." Ryk rubbed his neck. "Adrian blasted clear?" The *Ravid* had still been on the ground when he'd left. At least his cousin had exercised good sense and not left the night before.

"He did. Couldn't wait to reach Zeth to pick up his bride."

"Wonder what bride price he paid."

"He wouldn't say."

"For a healer it would be steep."

"No doubt." T'ganths had once approached the Talon clan leader about what the bride price would be for her. Jehna had turned down the suitor and they'd left disappointed.

"Regret not accepting a bid for you, cousin?"

Her cousin knew her too well. "No."

"What about you, Ryk? Do you intend to seek a bride?"

He sighed. "Not anytime soon."

Chapter 12

Harrison shaded his eyes as the Rover ship lazily dropped through the atmosphere and hovered near the spot Jehna Talon had once landed. The hatch opened and the man he recognized as Ryk Sargol walked out leading an almost blue-black colored horse. The others followed; their tails brushing their back and hindquarters.

"They're beautiful," Lissa commented, her fingers intertwining with his.

"They are," he agreed, giving her a warm smile. "Want a closer look?"

She nodded.

They crossed the ground and the Rover captain handed Harrison the rope. "They're all yours."

He released Lissa's hand as he led the horse to the corral attached to the barn. The other horses followed. They ranged in colors of brown and black. Thick sturdy legs and no doubt the membranes he'd suggested to protect their noses from the rain and snow. Eight total.

"You chose your two?" He glanced at Ryk who closed the gate after the last horse entered.

"I did."

"Fair enough." He removed the lead rope and the horse galloped away, the others joining the stallion. "Since they're here I'm assuming there weren't any issues."

"Never is. Not the first time we've picked up a load to deliver."

"Not always horses I'd bet."

"The breeders have much they trade in."

Lissa stood at the fence, her glowing eyes fixed on Harrison.

"How are the dogs and cats?"

"Settling in." The female cat birthed five kittens and the children were wanting them as pets. He'd tried to explain their function to catch rodents, but the youngsters had sulked, accusing him of being mean.

"And your brides?"

"I think most will be wed before winter ends."

Lissa gave him a look. "So you men think."

He shrugged. "Hungry Captain Talon?"

"I appreciate the invitation. On my flyover I noticed a storm brewing. I'd like to get landed before it strikes. Another time?"

"Agreed."

As he climbed over the fence, he watched the Rover return to his ship. The ramp retreated and the hatch closed behind the man.

"He's good looking." Lissa sent Harrison a teasing glance.

"Rovers rarely select a spouse outside their clan." Or so rumor said.

She shuddered. "Sounds awful."

With a shake of his head he placed an arm around her. "They may all be of the same clan…" How could he explain? "They're not all related to each other."

"What an odd way to live."

"It's worked for them for centuries."

~ * ~

The *Starrite* berthed near the other ships. Jehna watched from the fixed gate. Holly and Forrest had repaired the hinges, happy to discover the thick wood hadn't been damaged.

Ryk hurried across the field just as the clouds released their bounty. Jehna joined him and his daughter as they went inside.

"Not sure I like the rain." Tuleh shook out her cloak and hung it next to the door.

"There's a fire burning and I'm sure if you ask, Denebie would provide some hot cof."

The young woman nodded and ducked into the main living area.

"You two should pick rooms before the Wellers arrive," Jehna suggested.

"Good idea." Ryk walked with her to the fireplace, warming his hands. "How soon before they do?"

"Not sure. I'm sure when Adrian secures his bride, he'll head for Ronia."

"With the rest of his family not far behind." He accepted a cup of cof from his daughter, who took a seat on the floor.

"At least Roury will have others to play with," Tuleh added.

"Always a good thing," her father agreed. He met Jehna's eyes. "We'll have a difficult time meeting bride prices."

"Luckily, we won't have too many unbraided." She turned her back to the sizzling fire. "Trades can always be made."

"It's possible." Her cousin sipped his hot cof. "Three healers with services to offer."

"Two," Jehna corrected him. "I am or I will be clan leader."

"Altair has a daughter," he reminded her.

"Still a child." Although healer training started almost at birth. Jehna knew since her mother had done that for her.

"Roury at this age should be apprenticed."

"He's lived another life," she reminded Ryk. "He may not want it."

"Or he might."

"Not a decision we can make until we talk to his mother."

"Agreed." He took another drink. "Tuleh, how about we take a look at the upper levels and find us some quarters."

"Can we bring Topaz and Sapphire?"

Jehna smiled. She doubted the two Felcats would want to leave the *Starrite*.

"You know they may not want to," Ryk reminded his daughter.

"I know." She sighed and got to her feet.

"Come with me." He placed his mug on the table. "I'm guessing, cousin, you've picked yours?"

"First room on the next level." She glanced at her cousins. "There are stairs leading to a higher level. You might want to see for yourselves."

"Good suggestion."

Father and daughter left, leaving Jehna alone. She listened as the fire popped and enjoyed the warmth.

"He's a man who should marry," Denebie commented, picking up the empty mugs.

A brief vision flashed through her mind too quick for her to catch it. She rubbed her eyes. "He loved deeply. To do so again would be painful for him."

"Humpf," Denebie answered. "Any woman worth the Arkon's treasure would be a fool to turn down a man like Ryk Sargol."

"Only if the Arkon's treasure is as rich as the stories say."

~ * ~

With Tuleh's help Ryk offloaded the two horses and settled

them in the building that looked as if it had been set up for livestock. While she settled them into the stone stalls, he opened the doors on the other side. He smiled at the discovery. A tall unbroken fence extended out giving the animals plenty of pasture.

"I wonder if the previous occupants had horses," his daughter mused, coming to stand beside him.

"We have no way of knowing." His eyes studied the mountains in the distance shrouded with heavy clouds.

"Jehna mentioned there were ruins there." His daughter leaned against the building crossing her arms over her chest. "Might be worth letting the Shellmasters know."

"Be a lucrative trade," Ryk agreed. Often in the past the treasure seeking dragons had shared technology with the Rovers. One of the results were the highly advanced ships they flew.

"Too bad they've never figured out who originally built the ruins that have been explored."

He glanced at Tuleh. "As we've learned, we aren't the first who traveled the stars."

She rolled her eyes. "Tell me what I don't know."

With a laugh Ryk returned to the structure, his daughter following. "The horses need to exercise."

"Good idea." They'd been restless on the ship. Quietly and from long practice they worked together to release the horses. The pair dashed across the ground exploring their new domain.

He closed the doors. "We'll bring them in before night falls."

She nodded, heading toward the *Starrite*.

"Tuleh," she stopped to look at him. "I wondered, have you found anyone you're considering being braided to?"

A faint flush colored her cheeks. "Sort of," she replied.

"Oh?" First he'd heard of it.

"Mikhal and I have…reached an understanding."

Mikhal! Uncle Daniel's and Aunt Taeia's son. "Has he discussed this with his parents?"

She shook her head. "He wanted to wait until I became of age."

Wise move on the young man's part. Ryk would need to start considering a bride price. He gave his daughter a teasing smile. "What should I ask of him?"

"Dad!" A flush shaded her face.

"My daughter is worth much." Female Rovers were rare enough

and he'd been fortunate to have one.

She threw him an embarrassed look and ran toward the ship. He laughed and followed, wondering what exactly he should ask for her and how he'd manage to run his craft on his own without her help.

In the back of his mind he asked himself why he'd never rebraided and he pushed the thought away. He knew why and swore when his life mate died he'd never love another. Why now did that seem such a foolish thing to have done?

Chapter 13

"You're sure you don't want to come?" Jehna glanced at the group standing at the gate. All three of the Wayas, Altair and Arissa, plus Denebie and Roury.

"Someone needs to stay and look after the horses," Denebie replied. Roury grinned up at his mother.

"My services are always needed." Altair looked at the others. "I will start a garden."

Jehna understood what the healer meant. Plants and herbs could be used to heal plus flavor foods prepared for meals. She'd learned those as well, but hadn't had time to cultivate any. A part of her missed using her training.

"Next braiding," Demtrie promised. "I suspect our presence might cause some issues since I know the other clan leaders don't agree with this household."

He unfortunately had a point. Jehna knew from her contacts with Daniel most of the other clan leaders disagreed with the need for a new Homefall. "May the All Knowing One watch over you."

"And the Great Mother bless you," Altair returned.

She gave a head bow to those staying behind and headed for her ship. Tuleh skipped ahead excited about the braiding. Ryk fell into step beside her. "Once we get everyone here, our home may seem a bit crowded," he observed.

"We had more living on Ronia and we know all those who are joining us."

"True cousin."

"Besides there's plenty of room." They'd only occupied a small portion of the large dwelling. She glanced up and suddenly saw the landing field full of ships from all the clans. She shook her head and saw a scant few hovering.

"You all right?"

She sighed. Her mother had warned her the true sight ran in their family. Jehna had hoped it would skip a generation. That evidently wasn't the case. "Fine." She honestly didn't want to see events before they happened.

Ryk frowned knowing no doubt not to ask. "Easy journey."

"Easy journey," she returned.

~ * ~

Ronia's landing field was full with Talon and Jovan ships. Jehna landed *The Lady* on the edge of the field, the *Starrite* hovering next to hers. During the journey she'd changed into a fitted long-sleeved dress with a modest neckline, the shimmering fabrics complimenting her figure.

Before she exited her ship, she touched the necklace her mother had given to her. Much as she wanted to appear as a Talon at the braiding, she knew for this day, she must give honor to her abilities as a healer and appear as one. Tanner and Dannon followed her down to the hot sands, Hawk taking to the sky.

"Cousin." Ryk met her as Tuleh raced toward the house.

"Cousin." She'd seen his gaze sweep her dress. "You'll cause talk."

He chuckled as they walked through the maze of ships. "Uncle Daniel would like nothing better."

"We both know we're not suited for each other," she reminded him, watching as Dannon and Tanner disappeared inside where she'd lived much of her life. No doubt they'd find a cool spot and wait for the ceremony to begin.

"Tuleh informed me she and Mikhal have reached an understanding."

They'd reached the open gate and she stopped. "She's not of age yet."

"Not yet," he agreed. His eyes drifted over the ships. "We all knew from childhood Mark and Gem would braid."

"And now they have two ships and four children." Three boys who got bossed around by their older sister. Roury was going to love his new playmates.

"I'm surprised Altair and Arissa didn't come. They have no clan ties."

"I sensed she had a reason, but didn't want to talk about it."

He nodded and they entered the courtyard. Many of the cousins had arrived including the Wellers. Lonn Talu and Torey Gi'an, both the same age and had grown up as brothers. They flew the *Aralon*. Blood cousins Ryyk and Lon Talon, who flew the *Talon 7* and *9*. The older uncles who both had ships, yet seemed to prefer being grounded, working on projects around the compound.

Jehna recognized the Jovan clan chief Andron. With him stood a silver haired older man and a pair who looked like brother and sister. They stood talking with Daniel. Taeia Jehna didn't see and figured her aunt was probably with the bride getting her ready for the braiding.

"Uncle Daniel," she greeted.

"Jehna," he returned.

Andron gazed at her, a not quite friendly look on his face. "I'm surprised Altair and her daughter didn't attend."

"My apologies they didn't," she answered. He knew about the healer and her daughter. "They're still settling into their new home."

"I see." He turned to the older man. "This is Nickolai, my father and my blood cousins Ronik and his sister Marie."

"Welcome to Ronia." She inclined her head.

Nickolai narrowed his eyes. "A healer?" He turned his gaze to her Uncle Daniel. "You chose a healer as a leader of a new Homefall?"

She started to speak, but Daniel shook his head. "She's an excellent leader, pilot and healer. There's nothing that says she must choose one over the other."

"Humpf." His disapproval was written all over his lined face.

Her Aunt Taeia entered the courtyard and motioned for Daniel to join her. "Time to begin." He graciously led the way with the Jovan's following.

Ryk leaned toward her. "Not exactly friendly."

"We'll talk about this later." She knew well what the clan leaders thought.

~ * ~

Ryk found his daughter with Gem and Mark's children. She had them sitting on a shaded bench and thankfully quiet. Their parents stood next to them, holding hands. Errl stood next to his brother and their blood cousin Aaron winked at the kids who giggled. Mark glared at him.

The Jovans stood near their cousin, Shala Cambrie, if he remembered correctly. The young dark-haired woman with brown eyes tinged with green, stood in a long gown of brown with green markings. Adrian wore their clan colors of black, with intertwined orange and green stripes. The warm breeze ruffled his brown hair and his golden-brown eyes saw only his bride.

"Make a striking couple," Jehna said softly.

He glanced at her and nodded. "They do."

Uncle Daniel took his place, Aunt Taeia at his side. "We are here to witness the braiding of Adrian Colon and Shala Cambrie of the Talon and Jovan clans."

Andron shifted, yet did nothing, much to Ryk's relief. Despite Adrian meeting the bride price, he had the feeling the clan chief might not have fully supported the braiding.

The clan chief nodded and each pulled a silver wrap off their little finger. Adrian gathered a lock of Shala's hair, braided it and secured it. She then did the same for him.

"So witnessed," the clan chiefs said together.

Everyone echoed their words, moving forward to congratulate the newly braided couple. What would follow would be an evening of feasting, music, dancing, and catching up with his cousins.

"Ryk," he felt Jehna's fingers touch his arm. "Never miss a space window."

He gave her a surprised look as she moved away to stand beside Aunt Taeia wondering why she'd spoken those words to him.

~ * ~

"Your plan to start a new Homefall is not sustainable."

Jehna heard the words spoken by Andron Jovan and stopped outside her uncle's com room the morning after the braiding ceremony.

"If we're to overcome what happened years ago we must take risks," her Uncle Daniel countered.

"Crazy. To appoint a woman who is also a healer." She recognized Nickolai's voice.

"I have my reasons."

"No doubt," Andron continued. "I have heard the Weller's decided to join the Homefall. That is *not* what I wanted for Shala."

"I understand your concern." She heard a rueful laugh. "The Weller's have always been unpredictable and head strong."

She knew that was true. Taking a deep breath, she knocked and entered, pretending to be surprised to find the Jovan's there. "I'm sorry. Am I interrupting?"

"No." She didn't miss the look Uncle Daniel gave the Jovans.

"Anything happens to my niece," Andron began.

"She's going to fine," Jehna interjected before her clan chief could answer. "In fact I welcome having another woman who is also trained as a healer."

Andron stiffened.

"I understood it was her decision," Jehna said diplomatically.

The two Jovan men exchanged a look. Nicolai had been clan leader and had given the position to Andron. Made her wonder how much influence the older man still had.

Another knock and Errl entered, hesitating when he saw the Jovans.

"You obviously have clan business to attend to." Andron turned to look at her uncle. "We can continue our discussion later, Daniel Talon."

"Consider it completed."

They stared at him and left, their anger a distinct presence in the room.

"What was that about?" Errl asked, leaning against the wall, his arms crossed over his chest. His black hair short and trimmed, his brown eyes dancing with amusement.

"Not your concern." He turned to Jehna. "I need to talk to Errl."

"I know the discussion you want to have, and I should be part of it."

Her uncle hesitated before he nodded in agreement. "Errl, why didn't you discuss with me that the Wellers intended to join the new Homefall."

The other shrugged. As Jehna recalled, he was maybe two cycles younger than Daniel. "Intended to." He grinned. "Adrian decided to get braided and didn't seem the right time."

Daniel didn't suppress his laugh. Jehna grinned.

"I understand." He looked pointedly at Errl. "You find a bride yet?"

Trying to look innocent, Errl replied, "Who me?"

"Two of the four Weller men are braided. Wondered if you'd considered it."

"Nah." He pushed away from the wall. "Take quite a woman to tame me."

Why did Denebie flash through her mind? Roury needed a

father and Errl had basically raised his brother, cousin and Adrian, with Daniel and Taeia's help. Not to mention he adored his nephews and niece.

"All things in their time," she reminded her uncle.

He frowned, yet didn't ask. "It would have been nice to have been told."

"You will tell me if you decide to stay at my Homefall." Jehna tried to sound stern. Hard to do with her playful cousin who used to tell her bedtime stories.

"As you wish." Errl gave her a playful wink. "If you'll excuse me, I need to take what few belongings I keep here and put them on my ship."

Uncle Daniel motioned him away, staring thoughtfully at the door after Errl had left. "He's never braided."

"I suspect he won't stay that way."

Chapter 14

More ships on the landing field. Jehna wasn't sure quite how to feel about it. Seeing the *Clln, Pride, Cresent* and *Anybody's Guess* gave her hope for trades and sustaining the new Homefall. The children's laughter added a full future and briefly she saw a flash of a man standing beside her, holding her hand.

Shaking her head she concentrated on getting the Wellers settled. Mark and Gem found a dwelling large enough for them all and not connected to the main building. Errl and Aaron took up residence in a smaller one next to them. Adrian and his bride, another place close to the group, but slightly apart with space for a garden and a very large tree for shade.

"Shala has training as a healer," Altair told her when Jehna sat down to finally eat the soup Denebie had prepared along with a cup of tea. The warm room relaxed her muscles and she looked forward to a peaceful sleep.

"Fully trained?" she asked as she ate.

"Trained enough. She'll be helpful."

Jehna paused. "Can you train her alongside your daughter in what she doesn't know?"

Altair hesitated, her eyes following Forrest as he came in, taking a seat at the other end of the table. He rubbed the back of his neck and Denebie served him a hot cup of cof. "I could."

"It would help."

"You're fully trained." Altair focused her attention on Jehna.

"My mother and Aunt Taeia saw to that."

"The Arvona herself." The healer sounded both impressed and a little awed.

"She is Uncle Daniel's wife."

"They had a son from what I heard."

"Not unusual for Rovers."

"Have you ever wondered, from those long-ago days, why such things happen?"

Knowing to what the other referred, Jehna shrugged. "The politics of our ancestors hardly concern us now."

"Their outcome continues to."

"The Rovers chose another path." They were no longer mercenaries. Instead, they'd learned the secrets of trading and were considered better pilots than those who served the Arkon.

"Only because it was better than death."

She pushed her bowl away and sipped her tea. "That was before
any of us were born and are stories we tell our children."

"In all stories there is a partial truth."

"Not one we need to explore." Time to change the subject.
"Thank you for being willing to take over Shala's training."

"Of course." Altair rose, casting another look at Forrest. "Rest
well."

"Rest well," Jehna returned, as the healer left to go to her room.

Forrest moved to sit across from her. "What was that all about
and why the interest in the Rover's past?"

"Because as mercenaries we defended the Wise Women against
the Arkon. That's why they're so willing to intermarry."

"I thought it was because they can only conceive daughters
while we only father sons."

"I suspect that is part of it." There had to be more. She'd asked
Uncle Daniel and Aunt Taeia if there was. They'd only said many of
the early records had been destroyed.

"Don't see your shifters about."

"Hawk decided he'd rather stay with the horses and hunt the
rodents. Tanner and Dannon are patrolling."

"Predators?" He finished his cof, drumming his fingers against
his mug.

"Only ones I know about are the dragons. I doubt they'd be
fool enough to take them on."

"Dragons." Forrest shook his head. "Not like the Shellmasters?"

"Similar in appearance, but not intelligent."

"Took a trip up to the ruins."

She glanced at him surprised.

"Doesn't look like they've been explored or that anything has
been there since they were abandoned."

"I'll keep that in mind."

"Good profit." He smiled.

Forrest wasn't bad looking and she wondered if Altair held an
interest in the young man. "Always is."

~ * ~

"Morning cousin," Errl greeted as he sat down at the table.

Ryk returned the greeting. "You're up early, Errl." He took another bite of his breakfast. Eggs were a treat and he wondered how Denebie had managed to get a few chickens. She'd been vague about it and what she'd traded for them. She placed the hens in a small pen near the horses.

"I haven't met you yet," Denebie said as she plunked a plate in front of his cousin. "I'm Denebie."

"Errl," the older man answered, glancing at their cook and taking a second look. "Didn't see you last night when we landed."

"You were busy finding a place to live." She stepped back and smiled. "There's always food in the kitchen and hot cof. Feel free to help yourself."

"I will." Errl watched her as she left then asked. "She braided?"

"No." Ryk tried to hide his smile. His cousin rarely looked further than the night ladies. "Has a son."

"Yeah?"

"I don't know much. Denebie came with the women we brought as wives for Harrison Talbot. Her son is part Rover. I don't know which clan." Although he suspected Jehna knew.

"Huh." Errl chewed his eggs.

Ryk decided to leave well enough alone. If Errl was interested in Denebie he could manage on his own.

~ * ~

Several days had passed since they'd returned home from the braiding. Ryk worked at cleaning the hold since Tuleh was caring for the horses.

"Ryk!" Jehna's voice carried even to the lower levels.

"Be there momentarily," he called back.

"Sorry to disturb you," his cousin apologized when he joined her. "Got a message from Harrison. One of his neighbors would be interested in trading for wives."

"Oh?" He stepped outside to take a breath of air. She followed.

"I sent a message to Tamzin."

"Demtrie has the com up?"

She nodded. "I checked this morning."

"We'll need it."

"Agreed." Taking a deep breath she continued. "I want you to take Aaron and pick up as many brides as both your ships can carry. I suspect once the word spreads, we'll be able to make some trades."

"No doubt." He'd have to figure out how many he could safely carry and what supplies he'd need. Aaron as well.

"We're also invited to his wedding."

"Found a woman he likes." In the short time he'd gotten to know Harrison, he'd come to respect the rancher.

"We've met her."

"Reminds me, where did you put the cats?"

"They're in the barn. The female had five kittens."

"Wonder where Adrian found them," he mused. The younger man said he'd traded with an Earth colony, but hadn't shared which one.

"Where do we find anything when needed?" She smiled, glancing down. "It'll take Tamzin time to gather the women, so we'll be able to attend Harrison's wedding first."

"When is he getting married?"

"In a few days."

"Sure he isn't going to mind a bunch of Rovers showing up."

"Errl, Mark and Gem are leaving for a trade run. Adrian and Shala are going too. Forrest and Holly are returning to Tal to attend a braiding ceremony."

"Surprised their clan chief will allow them to."

"So far, he's the only one who supports Uncle Daniel."

"Demtrie's not going?"

"He's staying grounded."

Not often a Rover did that. No doubt the reason was a good one. Light rain started to fall and he wanted to go back inside his ship. "Anything else Jehna?"

"I contacted the Shellmasters to let them know about the ruins. They promised to be in contact with us soon."

Soon could mean immediately or several cycles. The dragons didn't measure time the same way humans did. "It's a start."

"We have things to discuss like when to plant crops and start orchards. Those are the products I'm thinking of trading for in exchange for brides."

"Good idea." The rain began to fall harder. "You should head back."

"I know." She took a step away. "Ryk, I haven't said anything to Aunt Taeia, but I have the true sight. I wanted to let you know."

"What have you seen?"

"Nothing that makes sense." She hurried away.

Ryk entered his ship, the Felcats looking up at him. "You don't like rain remember?"

Rain is fine. Getting wet is not. They trotted away.

He chuckled. Not often they deigned to speak. In the meanwhile, he needed to finish cleaning the hold if he planned on carrying brides to ranchers and their hands who wanted wives.

Chapter 15

Ryk saddled the horses, securing the saddles and the bags filled with food Denebie had prepared. Jehna entered the barn and nodded her approval. "Still remember how to ride?" he teased.

"Well enough."

"Denebie feeling any better?" The woman hadn't felt well for a couple of days and Altair had ordered her to bed for the rest of the day.

"She will. Not happy about missing the wedding." He watched her fingers slide down the horse's neck as she spoke to the animal. "Roury is staying with his mother."

"Too bad. I know he was looking forward to seeing his friends." All the boy had talked about was seeing everyone.

"His mother didn't want to burden us with watching after him."

"That's not how clans work."

His cousin smiled. "I'm well aware. Give Denebie time."

Tuleh entered, handing her father his cloak. "Still not coming?" He waited for her answer.

"Someone has to do the cooking with Denebie not feeling well. Altair doesn't know how and Roury needs me to look after him." She shrugged. His daughter didn't seem unhappy.

"Once we leave there's no changing your mind."

She rolled her eyes. "There are others here who will starve if I don't."

"Well," he conceded, "you are a good cook."

Tuleh grinned before hugging her father tightly. "Be careful."

"Always."

"Dannon and Tanner are staying behind and so is Hawk. They'll keep an eye out," Jehna promised as she mounted.

The teen frowned. "We haven't been threatened by anything."

"Nor do I think we will." Jehna turned to Ryk. "Ready?"

He nodded and put his foot into the stirrup, tossing his leg over. Took him a moment to adjust to the saddle and the horse took a step back. "We'll be home tomorrow at the latest."

"You better." Tuleh headed for the house, disappearing into the mist.

"Ready?" Jehna prompted.

"Ready." Giving a slight kick the horse moved and led the way through the early morning. The sky overhead hung with clouds. Thankfully it wasn't raining. Yet.

"We should be there before the ceremony starts," Jehna reassured him.

"And back before the sun sets?"

"Depends on how long you want to stay."

~ * ~

The bride had been whisked away to the dorm the night before and Harrison hadn't seen Lissa since. Molly fussed around the kitchen and from the wonderful smells, had made enough food to feed everyone on the ranch plus any additional guests who were coming.

He sat at his table forcing down hot cereal and hot cof. Soon he'd be wed again and he had to admit he had mixed feelings. Part of him felt like he was betraying his wife, while also telling himself she'd be happy for him. She'd want him to move on and have a good life.

The white cat sauntered across the floor, laying down in one of the chairs before the fireplace. A pink tongue worked to keep the fur clean and she paused to stare at him with yellow eyes. Lissa had wanted a cat for the house. He felt more comfortable with them outside. A small concession to make for the woman who had won his heart.

One of the children pounded on the door and opened it before he could invite them in. "Two horses coming in."

"Which way?"

"From the mountain trail."

Probably the Rovers. Harrison had been curious which two horses they'd kept.

"You going to greet them?" Molly asked, looking pretty in her blue gingham with a frilly apron. "Rovers no doubt made a special effort to get here."

"There only two people?" he asked the child.

"Yes, sir." The child rushed out the door, slamming it shut.

"They're bringing food to help out." Molly made shooing motions with her hands. "Go greet them."

"Yes, ma'am." He took his last swallow of lukewarm cof and

hurried out. The sun overhead peeked out behind the clouds. By nightfall there would be rain or perhaps snow, from the look.

Jehna raised a hand in greeting as they stopped in front of the house. "Hi, Harrison."

"Where's the rest?" He knew there were many living there and wondered where they were.

"We're not always at Homefall," she answered. "There are trades to be made." The Rover got out of the saddle. "Where's Molly? Denebie sent food."

"I'm here," the woman gushed, waving from the door.

He recognized Ryk who dismounted and handed the bags to Molly. "All you'll need to do is warm the food up."

"Denebie didn't come?"

He shook his head. "Altair confined her to bed for the day."

"Not serious I hope?"

"It's not," Jehna reassured the woman. "Denebie's been treated and Altair will keep a close watch on her."

"Good." Molly hurried back inside with the bags.

"Nervous?" Ryk grinned.

"A little." Harrison tugged at his shirt. "I need to finish dressing." The parson should arrive soon and he needed to be ready.

"I'll put the horses in the barn if that's okay." Ryk waited for his answer.

"Sure." He'd look at the animals later. Harrison hurried back inside. His jacket lay on his bed and he put it on. Fit a bit snug. Okay by him. The last time he'd worn it was when he'd married his wife.

~ * ~

Jehna joined the group gathering near the dorm. The hands took off their hats and held them nervously, each glancing at the various ladies standing at the front, who had dressed in the best clothes they had. Their dresses varied in faded shades of reds, blues and greens. Jehna had dressed practically in pants and top, her cloak thrown over her shoulders. The mountain pass had been cold.

Ryk came to stand beside her. "I don't like the look of those clouds."

"We won't stay long," she promised.

His eyes watched a group arriving. One of the men spotted them and brightened. "There's trading to be done," he observed.

Her hand rested on his arm. "After the ceremony."

A lean man in a long coat exited the dorm and stood outside. She watched Harrison scurry across the ground to take his place. A few moments later the door opened and Lissa walked outside. She wore a simple cream-colored dress and she smiled brightly at the rancher.

She joined him in front of the man who must be the parson. Harrison took her hand and the couple looked at each other.

"We're here for a wedding," the parson announced. "Harrison and Lissa want to be wed. Anyone object?"

Silence followed his question.

"Good. Hard part is done." He turned his attention to the couple. "You two want to get hitched."

"Yes," answered Harrison.

"Yes," echoed Lissa.

"So you be. Creator bless you both." The man grinned. "Let's eat."

Laughter rippled through the crowd. Jehna watched Ryk slip away and talk with some of the other ranchers she hadn't met. A line formed while several of the women helped Molly serve up food.

After getting a bowl of hot soup and a cup of tea, Jehna retreated to the barn to eat. One of the cats rubbed against her leg and she scratched behind the feline's ear. Kittens scampered through the hay under their mother's watchful gaze.

She'd finished eating by the time Ryk joined her. "How was the trade?"

He grinned broadly. "For more brides, we'll get fruit tree starts, seeds…" he paused to drink some cof. "Several baskets of already harvested vegetables and fruits." He dug into his soup. "Plus some of the local grain that thrives here."

"You made a very good trade, cousin."

"Had a brief conversation with Harrison."

"Really?" She thought the man would be too busy with his bride and well-wishers.

"Wanted to warn us the early signs indicate there might be one more heavy snow, possibly more, before the thaw comes and we can start planting."

Jehna knew all about watching nature for a hint about the weather. She appreciated the warning. "I assume you thanked him."

"Of course."

Rain began to fall. She could hear it on the roof. "We'd better get moving."

Ryk finished his food and nodded. "Going to be heavy rain according to Harrison. Said we'd better get moving if we want to get over the pass."

~ * ~

The ride home was miserable and wet. When they arrived, Ryk ushered Jehna into the house to warm up as he dried off the horses, put away the riding gear, and fed the animals. He hurried to the house, pausing at the gate when he thought he saw something move.

Through the heavy downfall a shape moved, a giant head swinging back and forth. He took a step toward it, when he felt a heavy body stop him. With a start Ryk recognized Tanner who urged him inside. As he closed the main door the wolf shook himself dry and trotted into the main living area.

Logs sizzled and popped, the warmth produced not piercing his soaked cloak.

"Get that off, father," Tuleh groused. "Hang it by the door and take off those wet boots."

He stared at his daughter, following her instructions, wondering when and where she'd learned a commanding tone. Seated at the table she served him rolled vegetables in a flat cake plus a cup of cocacof. "Where's Roury?"

"Asleep in his room. His mother is feeling much better, but Altair told Denebie to stay in bed another day."

"And our healers?"

"Far as I know Arissa and Altair are both in their rooms."

"Jehna?"

"She took a hot bath and I took up a tray for her." His daughter sat down opposite him. "I know you're second in command, but you don't need to keep track of everyone."

He took a bite, chewed and swallowed before answering. "I saw a creature in the rain."

Her eyes darted to the fireplace where both Tanner and Dannon had settled. "They're not giving a warning."

"No." He took a drink of sweet bitter mix. "I wanted to investigate, and Tanner stopped me."

"Smart wolf." She stretched. "What trade is next?"

"More brides for the ranchers."

"None for you?"

He blinked. "I have no desire to be braided."

"Sure." His daughter didn't sound like she believed him. "Once I'm braided, who is going to help you on the *Starrite*?" She got up. "Just leave your dishes in the sink. I'll get them in the morning." Tuleh left.

He sat for a time pondering the question she'd presented. Mikhal had his own ship the *Talon 8*. She'd be flying with Daniel's son.

Question was, and he knew it needed to be answered, was whether or not he wanted to be braided again.

Chapter 16

"Ready to go Aaron?" Ryk sat down at the table with the younger Rover.

"As I'll ever be." He sighed sipping his cof. "Why did they have to ask for brides?"

"It's a lucrative business and Jehna talked to Tamzin before the sun rose. She has a hundred women ready to leave Aris and resettle in the wilds of the nebula."

"Good thing both our ships will accommodate them." Aaron ate his last bite, chewing slowly as if savoring the flavor. "How many different ranches?"

Ryk did a quick check of his list. Five ranches in all had made deals. They could drop twenty women and any children there might be, at each. "We'll both take two ranches, make the delivery, and then meet at the last before we head back."

"Works." Aaron drummed his fingers on the table.

"You could have gone with the others." Ryk wasn't going to ask directly about why the youngest Weller hadn't gone with his cousins.

"On occasion, we make our own trades."

He understood that. "We should leave before the rain starts again."

With a curt nod they both left the table, deposited their dishes in the sink, grabbed their cloaks and headed for their ships. Ryk frowned as they stepped outside. One long wide imprint in the mud along the outside wall. A flash caught his eye and he picked it up.

"What's that?" Aaron eyed the find.

Turning it over in his hands, Ryk could feel the rough brightly colored scale. He remembered Jehna talking about the dragons who lived in the mountains.

"Dragon scale?"

"Maybe." He looked around wondering if that had been the shape he'd seen. "Let's get going."

Prepping his ship was easy and Tuleh had opted to join him. Jehna had promised she'd take over the cooking until Denebie felt better.

"We ready to lift?" His daughter stood in the control room, hands on her hips.

"Ready."

His fingers on the amber orb, he eased the ship up, through the heavy clouds and out in space, one of the few places he ever felt truly at home.

~ * ~

Aris was much the same. Busy, crowded, no moon in the sky making the night feel suffocating. Ryk followed the pathways to Tamzin's, Aaron beside him, watching for any sign of trouble.

"Don't like it," Aaron muttered.

Ryk didn't either. Most wore an expression of hopelessness. As if life had stolen all they had and they were confined to wander the streets, eating what they could find and sleeping in places none should.

Entering the one place any could find sanctuary, he found the place crowded. Women, children, a few men, not the usual sort who sought out the services of those who lived on the second floor.

"Captain Sargol," the Charon woman greeted. She glided across the room wearing fluttering pink, a color not complimenting her feline features.

"Tamzin," he greeted. "What's going on?"

"Word has reached me the messengers have come." She showed the two men through the main room and into a small inner chamber with a curved seat.

"Are you sure?" Ryk felt his heart quicken. Could it be true? Had they finally come?

"On Charon. We watch. Wait. For a sign."

"So you don't really know."

Her eyes slowly blinked at him. "It could be no one else."

"What's happening here?" Aaron glanced uneasily at the cloth hanging over the door. "I've never seen the people like this."

"Fault of those who advise," she snarled. "Once before it was like this."

A chill traveled down his back. He suspected he knew when and hoped he was wrong. "How many cycles ago?"

"During the dark time." Her claws came out. "I have what you asked for. A hundred brides who wish a better life."

"Are they here?" Ryk couldn't imagine her place holding them all.

"Nearby. I have one who owes me a favor. Volunteered his warehouse to keep them unseen and safe."

"Show us." He sensed they needed to hurry.

"Not I. Another." Tamzin stepped beyond the fabric. Two heartbeats later she returned with a woman with light red hair and wearing a brown tunic. "This is Elaine. She will take you."

~ * ~

Hurrying back through the dark streets, Ryk kept a close eye behind them. As far as he could tell, no one followed or even showed interest. The streets oddly absent of the Arkon's soldiers making him uneasy.

Elaine paused by a door, knocked twice, waited and knocked once, before she entered. Ryk followed hoping they hadn't fallen into a trap. Aaron checked behind them and closed the door.

They stood on a platform looking down upon a dirt floor. Below women slept on blankets, a few with young children tucked in around them.

"They'll have more comfort on our ships," Aaron observed, looking down on them.

"Agreed cousin."

"We did the best we could." Elaine sounded offended.

Aaron shook his head. "We can't move this many through the streets. We'll be noticed."

"You won't. If stopped simply say you are moving part of the Arkon's new harem to the preparation chambers."

"What!" Ryk couldn't believe what he'd just heard.

"They're located on the other side of the planet." Elaine glanced below. "The Arkon has new women brought all the time. Nothing unusual about it."

His stomach twisted and suspected Aaron's had as well. "I don't like it."

"We need to get them off world quickly." Elaine descended the stairs.

Ryk looked at his cousin who shrugged. "Think of us giving these women a better life." Aaron followed the woman. Ryk took a deep breath and hoped they didn't end up forgotten in the dungeon.

~ * ~

Those on the streets kept their heads down and did not seem to notice them. Ryk hoped they didn't end up meeting any official parties, despite Elaine's reassurances none of the nobles or soldiers ventured out after the sunset.

Loading the women on the ships proved easy. After sleeping in the warehouse for several days, moving into the ships' hold seemed a better choice. They split the women between the two of them. Ryk also took those with children, leaving the single women to his cousin.

"Here are the coordinates for the two ranches you're to visit, the agreed upon trade terms and the one we'll meet at," Ryk told Aaron, handing him the needed contracts.

"Safe journey," Aaron wished him, before entering his ship, shutting the hatch and retracting the ramp.

"I guess I go with you." Elaine gave him the first smile he'd seen on her face. Older than he first supposed, probably twenty-five cycles, her eyes were a lovely shade of blue.

"Everyone settled?" He motioned for her to follow him as he closed up his ship and prepared to leave.

"As they can be," she answered.

"If you need anything, let me or my daughter know."

"Your daughter?" Elaine sounded surprised.

"Tuleh." He headed up the stairs to the control room. "Best get ready. Not expecting a hard lift off. Best be prepared. In case."

"Of course, Captain." She gave him a final look before going below.

Easing the ship up and off the planet, he set the course and headed for the Tushiti Nebula. Once there, no one could follow. Only the Rovers knew the secrets and how to navigate the currents and eddies to reach Saris.

"She likes you."

He hadn't heard Tuleh enter. "Who does?"

"The woman you were talking to."

"Tamzin told her to be our guide."

"She's a woman, Father or didn't you notice?"

"That's enough." He hoped his daughter was teasing, yet could tell she wasn't.

"You've got some time to get to know her."

"Don't you have duties?"

"Done." She grinned. "Should never miss a window."

Jehna had said the same thing and it caught him by surprise. "You been talking to our cousin?"

"No. You should eat. I'll make you a meal." She ducked out.

Ryk sighed and checked his course before retreating to their private quarters. The two Felcats were there, snuggled together sleeping. He wondered when the entire population would vanish again only to reappear when least expected.

"Here." Tuleh handed him a plate holding an assortment of vegetables and some fruit. "Eat."

He sat at the small table close to their built-in kitchen. Their private quarters had mauve curved couches, with two doors leading to their private rooms.

"You know," Tuleh went on, handing him a cup of cof and placing her own food in front of her. "I have no problem with you rebraiding, should you find someone."

"I don't know if I want to." He scooped up a bite and ate it. Rich flavors exploded in his mouth and he wondered where Tuleh had learned those skills and from whom.

"You're still young." She sipped her cocacof. "I always wanted some brothers or maybe another sister."

"You're making assumptions young lady."

She shrugged. "Father, one of the goals of a Homefall is to braid and increase our clan."

"You've been talking to Uncle Daniel." How many times had he heard the same phrase growing up?

"Aunt Taeia," she informed him.

"We have those who are unbraided." The two older uncles Jeremy and Assar came to mind.

She shook her head. "Father," she breathed. "You're not listening."

"Maybe I don't want to hear."

"Fine. I'll talk to Jehna when we get home. Maybe she'll talk some sense into you."

~ * ~

Dropping the brides off at the various ranches proved to be

simpler than Ryk would have suspected. The only one who wouldn't leave was Elaine. She always motioned another to leave who happily walked down the ramp and into a new life. At the third and final stop, she refused to disembark. "I made a hundred and one," she informed him. "I don't have to leave."

Deciding not to argue with her, he counted heads and discovered they had the exact number agreed to. Taking payment, he returned to the Homefall with supplies and an extra woman. Denebie helped Elaine find a room, delighted to find out the woman also liked to cook.

"You can help me in the kitchen." She began showing Elaine where all their supplies were kept.

Ryk found Jehna in the main room. The fire crackled and warmth dispelled the damp cold seeping inside.

"Came home with an extra I hear," Jehna turned to face him, her back to the fire.

He shrugged. "She made a hundred and one."

His cousin smiled. "Funny how the All Knowing One sets one on a path with a destination none expect."

Wanting to yell, he held his temper. "No one controls my path."

"I said nothing about control. Only choices set before us to decide what we truly wish or providing for our heart's desire we did not know we had."

"And what of you cousin?"

"The one I wait for has yet to arrive."

Chapter 17

Ugly gray clouds crowded over the valley dropping wispy flakes. Tuleh and Roury had gone out to make sure the horses had plenty of water and brought all the cats indoors. Hawk, Tanner and Dannon abandoned the barn as well and the three shifters settled themselves in the main room near the fireplace.

The cats ended up in a small corner of the kitchen. Denebie made a soft bed for them near the stove and placed dishes with water and leftover meat from the night before. "I haven't seen any mice in the house," she'd commented.

'I ate them,' Tanner informed Jehna when she'd joined them at the fireplace.

'You have our thanks.'

'They were nice snacks.'

Jehna laughed and rubbed behind his ears. Dannon sighed the way cats on occasion do, his back as close to the fire as he could get. Hawk found a perch high up on the chimney and settled in.

Ryk joined her with a smile. "Demtrie says the Wellers are about to land."

She knew snow wouldn't be an issue for the pilots. They'd had plenty of practice on various trade runs on other planets. Not all of them had sun and hot weather as they'd had on Ronia.

"How's Aaron doing?" she asked.

"He's fine." Ryk chuckled. "With half the family braided, and Errl interested in Denebie, I think he's a bit more lonely than normal."

"Are the Felcats still in the ships or have they resettled inside."

Ryk frowned. "I haven't seen any of them since early this morning."

"You think they vanished again as they tend to do every few cycles."

"I'm not sure."

'Tanner? Dannon? What say you?'

Dannon didn't deign to answer. Tanner on the other hand replied, 'Crystal vanished. No worry. She always comes back.'

'I know.' They'd never been able to get the Felcats to tell them where they went. The only answer she'd gotten was they'd gone home. Wherever that was and however they got there and back.

"Tanner says Crystal left."

"Means the other Felcats did as well." He rubbed the back of his neck.

"Living and dealing with other intelligent species means accepting their ways even if you don't understand them."

"Which lesson did Uncle Daniel include that bit of wisdom?" He grinned.

"No idea, but it's true." Their Felcat companions, who were both telepathic and intelligent, rarely shared their hidden world. Long ago she'd accepted their truth. Crystal stayed because Jehna respected their ways.

Cold air circled inside followed by loud talking, laughter and children's happy voices. "I'd say the Wellers have come home," Ryk observed.

"Good to have them. Any word on Holly and Forrest?"

"Demtrie says they're in route. Hopefully they'll land before the storm gets worse."

She nodded, aware the Wayas Homefall had a mix of seasons with snowstorms and heavy rains. "They'll be fine."

Errl took a seat at the table, his cousins and nephews and niece joining him. "What's for dinner?"

Denebie appeared carrying a large kettle. Immediately Errl was on his feet and took it from her, placing it on the sideboard. "You could have asked for help," he chided her.

"I can manage," she huffed back.

Elaine appeared carrying bowls. Mark and Gem followed Denebie back to the kitchen and helped serve the rest of the food. Hot fresh bread smell filled the room, along with the spicy soup, and other vegetables. Ryk and Jehna joined them.

"I'll take a tray up to Demtrie," Tuleh volunteered.

"Thank you." Denebie gave the young woman a smile.

Tuleh blushed.

"You raised a considerate girl," Denebie complimented Ryk.

"Had help."

They took a moment to thank the All Knowing One for their food. When they finished Altair and Arissa joined them, the healer glancing around the table. "Where's Forrest and Holly?"

"On their way home," Ryk answered.

"Oh." She quietly ate her dinner.

The room filled with stories as the Wellers shared their adventure. The children giggled and teased each other, Roury joining in the fun. Jehna relaxed and enjoyed the shared banter. Her Homefall would be successful. She knew it. Once again she saw a man at her side smiling at her. Before she could see his face he wavered out of her sight.

"Cousin?" Ryk's inquiry jarred her back.

"I'm fine." She picked up her cup and sipped her tea.

Cold seeped in again when Holly and Forrest arrived. They found places at the table, Holly next to Aaron and Forrest sat with Altair. Jehna found their choices interesting and decided not to comment, particularly since Denebie sat next to Errl and Elaine on the other side of Ryk.

How soon before the couples become braided and when would she meet the man she kept knowing would come?

~ * ~

Snow began to fall heavily as night fell, covering the valley with thick white, clinging to the bare tree branches and burying future garden spots. Mist oozed after it, embracing the house in chilly arms.

Jehna stood in the com tower staring down at the landing field. The ships hovered, becoming white on top while the area underneath escaped the increasing accumulation. Demtrie sat near the coms, cleaning some of the equipment, no doubt listening for any possible communications.

Forrest joined them, picking up his cousin's tray. "Anything I can get you?"

Demtrie shook his head. The young man nodded and she heard his boots on the stone stairs as he returned to the lower level.

"I think I'll do some work in my office." She had a small extra room next to her quarters she used to go over their profits, expenses and possible losses, a better place to go over the more boring aspect of her position as Homefall leader.

Later in the night a light knock roused her from the numbers and she called, "Yes?"

Forrest stuck his head in. "The dragons are here."

His words took a moment to register. "Wake the kids." She closed the ledger and went to her room to grab a thick blanket, joining the others as they hurried to the com dome. As they arrived, she could smell the sweet scent of a warmed fruit drink and the spicy aroma of a beverage the adults preferred. Denebie and Elaine had set up a table anticipating the fun and filled it with hot food.

Helping herself, Jehna grabbed a baked sweet roll and found a nice corner where she could watch the scene below. The children spread their blankets as close as they could to the large window and peered out, their giggles filling the large room.

The adults sat further back, even Demtrie joined them. They sipped their drinks and waited to see what the creatures did. They knew they were there, but had not yet seen them. Not totally true since she'd seen one when she scouted for their Homefall.

Three dragons frolicked in the snow. One had green scales and a bright blue feathery mane. Another wore a red mantle with matching scales. The last was a bit smaller, a brilliant blue with teal about its neck.

They dived into the snow, sliding across leaving a furlough before getting to their feet, scuttling back to their starting point, and repeating the process. They didn't seem to tire, although the children did. They fought going to sleep, but eventually, they succumbed and their parents and cousins carried them back to bed.

Denebie returned after she'd gotten Roury settled, although Mark, Gem and Altair did not. The rest stayed in the room until first light, when the dragons hurried off, disappearing into the rapidly falling flakes.

Forrest gently prodded Demtrie awake and helped him to his bed. "I'll watch the coms," he promised when his cousin protested.

Jehna and the others each grabbed empty plates and cups, plus leftover food and took them back to the kitchen. Denebie and Elaine took them and put away the extra.

"Don't worry about breakfast," Jehna told the women. "Get some rest. We can help ourselves if we're hungry."

The two nodded and headed for their rooms. Ryk gave her a smile. "You too. We've all earned some sleep."

"That includes you," she retorted.

"Of course." They laughed and found their respective beds, the house settling into a peaceful quiet and in the distance as she dropped into the land of dreams, a faint loud rumble reached her ears.

~ * ~

Late morning, when Jehna rose, found gray colored clouds hanging over their home dropping thick heavy snow. Hot cof waited, the rich smells filled the kitchen while she made herself some tea. She took a sweet bun from the night before and made her way to the table.

Heat embraced the room. The fire crackled and sizzled. She knew someone had been up earlier since several stacks of wood stood piled next to the stone fireplace. Dannon and Tanner still slept. Hawk had come down from his perch and seemed to be eating what she hoped was a mouse.

"Morning," Ryk mumbled as he sat down with a cup of cof and hot cereal. "Elaine made it earlier," he explained, as he took another bite.

"I trust she got some rest."

"Left it to simmer and went back to her bed." He stretched. "I got up earlier to check on the horses and chickens." He pointed in the direction of the fireplace. "Got some wood."

"Both of us, taking care of the Homefall."

"As we should." He sipped from his cup. "We have lots of seeds and starts."

"We'll need it." She swallowed a sweet morsel. "We just need to figure out who has enough knowledge to manage the planting."

"I can do that," Elaine told them as she sat next to Ryk. "My family had a farm before the noble—" She stopped, taking a deep breath. "Before we lost everything because we couldn't meet the tithe price."

"What happened to your parents?" Ryk asked quietly.

"I don't know. Lord Peppler took me as a servant for his house." She shivered. "I heard later he burned our home and those who feared for their lives whispered my parents were inside."

"Do you have other family?" If there were any siblings, Jehna needed to know so she could have Tamzin find them.

"No. My younger brother went to serve the Arkon. He ran away because my parents didn't approve and last we heard he'd been accepted. My sister," she swallowed. "I'm not sure what happened to her. She'd been at a friend's when they came for us."

"You're from Aris." Jehna had to be sure.

"The other side of the planet. That's where most of the farms are. Far from the Arkon's sight."

Ryk added a question. "How many cycles ago?"

"Five orbits."

"Similar to my story," Denebie interjected, sitting down, a cup of steaming cof between her hands.

"How so?" Jehna needed as much information as she could.

"The nobles have been taking farms when they can escape the Arkon's notice." She took a sip. "They took the place my parents left to me."

"Your," Ryk hesitated. "son's father?"

Denebie closed her eyes. "They didn't know about us." She glanced at her son, who sat gobbling hot cereal. "I was lucky I got Roury back. Tamzin helped." She shivered. "Children are sent to mines since they are small enough to get into places where adults cannot."

Jehna and Ryk exchanged glances. Both of them had heard the rumors which they had never been able to confirm.

"You're safe here," Ryk reassured Denebie.

Jehna wanted to ask more about Roury's father. In the future it might prove important to know. She sensed Denebie wasn't ready to talk about it. Nor was it uncommon for a Rover to father a son with a woman with whom they were not braided. Normally though, the woman let them know and the clan took them in. She'd forgotten to speak to Uncle Daniel about it during Adrian's braiding. Given the tension, maybe not mentioning it had been best.

"I should probably start food for the midday meal." Denebie rose.

"Can I check the horses?" Roury bounced up.

"I already did." Ryk must have noticed the boy's crestfallen expression. "Tell you what, why don't you check on the mother cat and her kittens and make sure they have enough food?"

Roury brightened and jumped up, running into the kitchen.

"Thank you." Denebie threw Ryk a grateful look.

"My pleasure."

The woman returned to her domain. Ryk glanced at his cousin. "What?"

"You definitely need to get braided again and have more

children."

Elaine made a choking sound. "If you'll excuse me." The woman hurried away.

"Subtle, Jehna."

"I see how she looks at you. Don't be blind." She leaned forward. "She'd be a good match."

"I'm not,"

"No more excuses. Your braided spouse died ten cycles ago and I know you loved her." She forced him to meet her eyes. "You have a huge heart, Ryk. There's room for another."

"Maybe." He grabbed his dishes and headed for the kitchen.

"Stubborn man." She shook her head and finished her tea.

Tanner lifted his head, his wolf eyes looking into her soul. 'And the one you see?'

'Yet to come.'

'Or has and you have not yet met.'

Could that be true? Jehna wasn't sure. In the following days, no doubt the discovery would be a surprise.

Chapter 18

"One of the Shellmasters arrived last night," Forrest informed Jehna when he brought a midday meal tray to her office.

"What?" She put aside her plans for where to start the orchards. Maybe the Shellmaster's ship landing had been the sound she'd heard just before she'd fallen asleep.

"Demtrie talked with the pilot this morning. A freelancer who agreed to bring the dragon here." He chuckled. "The Shellmaster seems quite eager to explore the ruins."

"He does understand the mountain passes can't be accessed?"

"We explained about the storm. The Shellmaster said he'd wait."

No doubt he would. The Shellmasters had very long lives and were never in a hurry. "He have a companion?" Most of them were accompanied by some sort of feline.

"Didn't ask, but I'd bet on it."

She would too. "Make sure they're comfortable. They'll have to stay where they are until the storm stops."

"Already did. They are. Although the old dragon seemed to enjoy talking to Demtrie."

Might be good for the older man to have some company. "I agree." Her nose detected some interesting spicy smells and her stomach reminded her she'd had a very light breakfast. "Thank you for the tray."

"Ryk said you were busy and would probably forget to eat." Forrest headed for the door, pausing before he left. "You have any issue with me courting Altair."

"Not as long as she's given her consent."

He grinned and closed the door. She giggled. Evidently the pair had spent more time together, which could happen during storms. Not much else to do except tell stories, play games, eat and sleep.

Taking a bite of the spicy vegetable dish, she ate slowly, enjoying the home cooked food. Her favorite was the bread, soft, warm and moist, melting in her mouth. She carried a piece to the slivered window, seeing only white. The storm must have gotten worse.

"At least we were warned." Ryk stood inside the door.

"I'll have to remember to thank Harrison."

"Forrest informed me of our guest."

"At least we know the Shellmasters are interested." She returned to her desk and sat down. The room was only large enough for it and a chair.

"Chilly in here."

"I know."

"You should join us in the main room."

"I have work to do."

"There isn't much you can do today." He cocked his head at the window. "Not with this storm." Ryk moved to stand before her desk. "Even Uncle Daniel mingled with family during the sandstorms."

"I remember." Those storms were some of her fondest childhood memories. The Talons all gathered in the main hall. Uncles Jeremy and Assar telling stories, while the children munched on sweet cookies and drank hot coca. Aunt Taeia hugging each of them and kissing their cheeks. They'd never let any of them know how dangerous the sands could be.

"We should give the children the same memories."

"You're right." Although she suspected the dragons' snow antics would be remembered.

He took her tray and she followed him down the stairs. The entire future clan had gathered near the fireplace. Errl telling stories to the children, while couples sat together holding hands. She took in the scene with a smile, another flash of a man beside her, his arm around her, a scent she did not know yet familiar enveloped her.

Ryk jolted her back to the present when he walked past, holding Elaine's hand. The woman's eyes betrayed how she felt and Jehna was happy for them both. Ryk just needed to put the past behind him and enjoy what he could have in the future.

~ * ~

Everyone sat around the table for dinner consisting of hot tatoes, with a thick spicy meat gravy, along with fresh bread, hot cof, or tea in Jehna's case or coca for the children. Laughter and conversation filled the room. When they'd finished, the youngsters sat on the floor, listening to another story Errl shared.

"A big giant appeared..." Errl stood up and she heard gasps. Her cousin was pretending to be the mighty enemy warrior in his tale.

Ryk hid a laugh behind his hand. "Errl's going to be a good father."

"He's had practice," she reminded him. Her eyes rested on Mark, Gem, Aaron and Adrian. His bride Shala helped clear the table. "We need to talk to Harrison to see when it might be safe to plant crops and get the orchard started."

"One project at a time." His eyes followed Elaine as she left the room.

"You could go help," she suggested.

He glared at her. "I'm not interested."

She gave him a look that said 'I know better.'

"Going to check on the horses," he grumbled, getting up and heading to the main door.

"Dad can be stubborn." Tuleh grabbed the bread platter. "He likes her."

"Just doesn't want to admit it."

"Pretty much." The young woman shook her head. "I already told him it's okay if he gets braided again. I'd love to have some brothers or a sister." She headed for the kitchen. Tuleh had a point. Even by Rover standards Ryk was still young. Average life span, from what she remembered, was around one hundred twenty cycles. How many more of them would they have had if the scourge of fifteen cycles ago hadn't happened?

~ * ~

Ryk paused when he heard raised voices in the hallway. The horses needed to be fed and watered and chicken nests checked for eggs. A morning routine he'd established weeks ago.

"What do you mean you're going to be the Shellmaster's guide?" Altair demanded, hands on her hips, her brown skirt nearly touching the floor.

"Just what I said," Forrest returned, pulling on heavy boots and grabbing his cloak. "I've done a couple of trips on the trails to the ruins."

"The snow is still too deep," she retorted.

Snow still fell and had been for several days. Temperatures hadn't risen much and Ryk wondered at the wisdom of taking the dragon up into the mountains. "What does the Shellmaster say?" he interjected, stepping into the entry.

"He's anxious to get started and doesn't care about the snow." He laughed. "He dug out around the ship. His companion, an orange tiger, rolled in it and ran around like a young cub."

"These temperatures can kill," he reminded the younger man.

"Shellmasters radiate heat. We'll be warm enough."

"Talk some sense into him, Ryk," Altair pleaded, her pale green eyes shimmering with unreleased tears.

Ryk took a deep breath. Jehna should be handling this situation, but she'd been up all night with an unexpected clan chief meeting. Denebie had fed her breakfast then sent her to bed.

"It's Forrest's decision." From the look on Altair's face, she hadn't expected his answer.

"I'm going." Forrest pulled his hood over his face. "The best part is this dragon flies. We'll get there in no time."

Furious, the healer stamped her foot and stormed away, muttering words in her native sing-song language. Ryk wondered what she'd said.

"Take care," he warned the younger man.

"We all take risks or we wouldn't have trades." Forrest slipped out and damp cold invaded.

"I'll have hot cof waiting for you," Elaine promised, her hand lightly touching his arm. Her expression reminded him of his wife when she'd been concerned about him.

"Thanks." He braved the chilly outside, taking care of the horses and gathering eggs from the chickens. He kept the basket inside his cloak to keep the shells from freezing, stomping his feet on the stone floor when he entered the main door.

Roury appeared and Ryk handed him the egg basket. "Give those to your mother." The boy grinned and dashed into the kitchen. He took off his boots and hung his cloak, padding into the main room and standing before the fire, the heat warming his body.

"Your cof." Elaine handed a cup to him.

He took it with a smile and drank the contents. The liquid warmed his insides. She stayed by his side, not making conversation, keeping him company. "Thanks."

"You're welcome. How do you like your eggs?"

"Doesn't matter."

"I'll make you some." She paused, squeezing his arm, before she left.

"You should braid with her." He turned, surprised to see Mark sitting at the table. The young man smiled, although with his scar it appeared a bit lopsided. "She'd be a perfect partner."

"Experience talking?" Ryk sat across from the younger man.

Mark shrugged. "Gem and I were lucky. We always knew we'd braid."

"Uncle Daniel make you pay the bride price?" Mark had never said and Ryk found himself curious.

He pursed his lips as if debating on whether or not to share. "He got a cut of our first cycles profits. Took us longer to get Gem's ship with the agreement and delayed us having children." He shrugged. "Worth it though."

"Always is." Ryk thought back to his first braid. He'd been so in love with Tuleh's mother Mirra. He'd been sixteen and planning on buying his ship when the sickness had swept through the Homefall. His parents like so many others had fallen ill within days. They'd quarantined in their quarters so it wouldn't spread.

Taeia had been there. Why he couldn't be sure. When Daniel's parents passed, his cousin had taken over leadership and the healer had agreed to braid with him. Their union had given strength and hope to them all.

His parents passed soon afterward and within a short time the older generation of Rovers were gone. The only survivors being uncles Jeremy and Assar. They'd been ill for a time, yet had recovered.

They'd learned all the Homefalls had been stricken. Only those who had just come of age and the young children survived. The next few cycles had been filled with rapid rebuilding to keep their home strong and flying so they could make trades.

Ryk had grown up with Mirra and had always been fond of her. She wasn't a blood cousin and they'd braided when Taeia declared the sickness gone. Their daughter had been born less than a cycle later. They'd planned to have more children, but with establishing trades of their own, they never had.

By Rover standards, he knew he was still young. Having more children was not out of the question. He glanced up as Elaine placed a plate in front of him with spicy meat and scrambled eggs, along with a hot biscuit.

"I'll refill your cof." She disappeared with his mug.

"Elaine is a good match." Mark pushed his empty plate away and finished his cof.

"You said that already."

"Just reminding you." Mark rose, dishes in hand. "I need to see to my ship and check on Gem and our children."

"Planning on having more?" Ryk took a bite of his eggs. Elaine had cooked them perfectly and just as he liked them.

"Off and on." Mark took off to the kitchen.

Elaine returned with his cof and gave him a smile. "Any plans today?"

"Other than keeping an eye on things so Jehna can rest?" He shook his head. "Often quiet during a storm."

She sat down next to him. "I've heard stories about the Rovers. Hard to know what is true and what isn't."

"There are lots of stories about us." Some dated back hundreds of cycles as he recalled.

"I'd like to know more." Her hand rested on his arm.

He couldn't decide if Elaine touching him was good or not, yet it had been many cycles since he'd had someone special in his life. Getting to know the woman couldn't hurt. If nothing else it would make working with her easier. "I think that can be arranged."

~ * ~

Harrison gazed at the Ghost Mountains, covered with clouds. The cold season rarely lasted this long and he hoped the Rovers had prepared well. He took a sip of hot cof and tried not to shiver. Not much could be done beyond checking on the livestock until the storms cleared. His foreman had taken a couple of hands to do that. They were back in the bunkhouse warming up.

"You should come inside." He turned to gaze at his wife. She stood just outside wearing a thick coat.

"In a few minutes," he promised.

"You shouldn't worry so about the Rovers. From what I've always heard, they're a hardy bunch."

"They are at that." He hadn't forgotten finding Jehna Talon at the top of the mountain with her companions and the encounter they'd had with the wild dragon. Selling the land to her for a new Homefall and her payment for it in brides had paid off. About half of his hands had married.

"I envy them their cloaks. Seem to keep them warm." His wife sounded wistful.

"Want me to trade and get you one?" He'd do anything for her.

"Not today." Her eyes looked upward. "You'd never get over the pass."

"Wouldn't be fool enough to try." He saw Lissa shiver and he ushered her back inside, helping her take off her coat. "You should get warm by the fire."

"There are better ways to get warm." Her eyes held promise.

Lissa was correct. He grinned. "You are certainly right."

Chapter 19

A quarter of a cycle passed when the heavy storms stopped finally. Clearer skies followed and with the warmer weather, everyone had helped plant the crops and start the orchards. If they had a successful harvest, they might be able to trade or sell the extra. Their efforts included both Jehna and Altair establishing herb gardens for healing and spices for their food.

Jehna looked up from gathering the first of the herbs, stretching out her tired back, as her gaze reached the sapphire sky. She sat back on her heels. Thick mist crept down the mountains and she knew they'd soon have drenching rain.

"Forrest come back yet?" Ryk inquired, kneeling down beside her.

"Checked in with Demtrie early this morning. The Shellmaster is excited about the discoveries he's made."

"Altair misses him."

"Forrest asked if I approved of his courting Altair before he left." She smiled at her cousin. "I agreed."

He gave her a look she knew meant she should have told him sooner. He nodded. "Figured you had."

She got to her feet holding the basket containing what she'd gathered. "At least we'll have a few new herbs." Good timing too since she'd learned Harrison's wife was with child.

Ryk stood, rubbing his neck. "What should I do about Elaine?"

"What do you want to do?" She'd watched the romance bloom between the pair. Elaine would be an excellent partner for Ryk. If he'd relax enough to accept what the woman offered.

"Ryk," she began. "Mirra is gone and has been for many cycles. I knew her well enough to know she'd want you to be happy."

"I never wanted to love again."

"What our plans are and what the All Knowing One knows is best for us, can at times be—" She struggled for the right words. "Unexpected."

"You must walk close to him."

"As close as I can. I'm less than perfect."

"I've heard rumors." He glanced around as if making certain they were alone. "That the messengers might have come."

"Where did you hear that?" A small reptile crawled across a branch and settled in the sun. The leathery white skin shimmered and huge golden eyes blinked closed.

"From Tamzin."

The Charon had mentioned the messengers the last time she'd visited. Tamzin might have a version of the true sight allowing her to see what others couldn't. "We knew they'd come."

"We've never known when."

She headed toward the main house. Ryk walked beside her under the deep purple leaves attached to copper branches. They followed a set stone path back inside through a side door.

"The designers of this place had an eye for beauty," her cousin commented.

"They certainly knew how to blend the stones." She'd walked over the ground they hadn't yet explored for several days, finding more private dwellings, plus what looked like a storage area large enough to contain what they could harvest. They needed a good and dry place to carry them through the cold season, if the one that had just passed was any indication.

"The Wellers checked in this morning. Mark and Gem will be back soon. Errl took Aaron with him to pick up the next load of brides."

"Errl mention anything to you about courting Denebie?" Jehna was curious if their cousin had expressed his intentions to Ryk.

"Not yet." He chuckled "He's never braided and I suspect he's not sure he wants to."

"I think he's never braided because he hasn't found anyone." She placed her basket on the table. Seemed odd not to have the familiar sound of the fire sizzling. "Most have before they reach thirty cycles."

"He delayed and you know why."

"We all do." He'd spent most of his time helping to raise his brother, blood cousin, Aaron, Gem and Adrian, plus apprenticing them all.

Elaine hurried out of the kitchen with two mugs. She handed one to Ryk and the other Jehna. "With your permission?"

"We can talk more later." She watched Ryk start to follow

Elaine before he stopped.

"One more thing. Tuleh and Mikhal plan to braid." He took a deep breath. "She told me last night."

Not a surprise. Those two had been courting before the new Homefall had been established. "She excited?"

"She is. Uncle Daniel contacted me for the bride price."

"What did you tell him?" She was curious what he thought his daughter was worth.

"That I'd let him know."

~ * ~

As Ryk worked in the barn, with the eager help of Roury, he wondered how much his daughter was worth. Bride price could be a specified amount and payable to the father, or a portion of profits or a trade. As clan leader, Uncle Daniel could afford to pay anything he asked for. Question being, what would be fair.

"I'm taking the eggs to mom," Roury said, holding up the basket so Ryk could see.

"She'll be happy to get them."

"I'm going to ask her to make a cake!" The boy walked briskly out into the sunshine.

He frowned. They really needed to find out which Jovan had fathered the child, unless Errl made up his mind and braided with Denebie. Then he could adopt Roury and none would ask the question.

Giving the horses some extra grain, he turned to find Elaine standing outside the stall, her hands on her hips. She wore a brown dress and her blue eyes flashed fire. "What's this I hear about selling your daughter?"

He sighed, understanding Elaine's confusion. "I'm not selling her."

"Then why is her future husband asking for a price?"

Taking a deep breath, he pointed to a bale and sat down. Elaine glared at him before sitting next to him. "Well?" she demanded, arms crossed over her chest.

"Daughters among us are rare and of great value."

"I'd heard—" she began, biting her lip, before speaking again. "Rovers only father sons?"

"As a rule, yes." He rubbed the back of his neck. "Something to do with our genetics. You'd have to speak with Jehna or Altair for a better explanation."

"Is it also true the wise women only have daughters?"

He nodded.

She looked away, her eyes traveling the lines of the barn. The kittens who had grown were playing with a mouse their mother had caught earlier and he smiled watching the hunting lesson.

"It's our custom," he further explained, drawing her attention back to her first question.

"Does marrying a wise woman increase the chances of having a daughter?"

"We're not sure."

"So most Rovers marry—"

"Braid," he corrected her.

"Fine. Braid with other women who aren't Rovers."

"If we're fortunate to find a woman." They'd braid with Rover women too, if they could find one.

Her hand rested on his. "Why do you keep this a secret?"

"Would you expose your greatest weakness for all to see?"

She took a moment to consider before answering him. "No. I suppose not." Elaine sighed. "I would love to have a daughter."

"With the All Knowing One, anything is possible." He smiled. "I would be happy with a son or another daughter."

"You want more children?" She sounded surprised.

Did he? Ryk couldn't be sure. "My wife and I had planned on having more." The normal sting he felt when he spoke of her failed to appear. Perhaps he was ready to move on. "Walk with me." He rose and extended his hand.

Surprised, she took it, her eyes questioning.

"We need to find Jehna. I need her permission to court you, if you're agreeable."

"Yes!" she squealed, throwing her arms around him.

He laughed, delighted she'd agreed. Ryk hugged her. They walked outside and toward the house. Jehna would be happy for him and she'd been right, the All Knowing One did provide what he needed and at the right time. For such grace, he was very thankful.

~ * ~

"How long is Forrest going to stay in the ruins!" Altair demanded, pacing the main room. "He should have come home already."

"You heard his report this morning," Jehna reminded the Wise Woman. "The Shellmaster made a discovery and isn't ready to return yet."

The healer wiped at her cheek. "I miss him."

Jehna had given the couple privacy when they'd spoken earlier and suspected Forrest missed Altair as well. "He speaks to you every time he checks in."

"Not enough," she grumbled, her eyes focused on the fireplace. "I want him here."

"We're being paid well for the service we're providing." Jehna knew the total of the agreed amount plus a stake in the discoveries made. Such had given them the advantage in the past and for the future. Their ships and navigation systems were two such.

"Trades. I swear by the Great Mother that's all Rovers think about."

"Family is important." Having been raised partly in a clan household, Jehna knew the truth. "Trading is how we live."

"Healing is how I live."

"Why did you join our household?"

"One of the other healers wanted Arissa for wife to her son. He's ten orbits her senior."

"What of her future?" Jehna knew as clan leader, one day she might have to bargain a bride price for the girl, once she came of age.

"She's a healer. That should be enough."

"On Sharmain, yes." She shook her head. "Not in a Rover household." Jehna raised her hand when Altair started to protest. "Wise women hold a different position inside the clan. Should your daughter one day wish to braid, the match will be discussed."

"You won't discuss it before then?"

"I promise I won't."

"Fine." Altair seemed satisfied. "I need to check on Arissa. See how she's handling the herbs."

"I'm sure you're teaching her well."

"I am." She tilted her chin. "I think you have someone else who wishes to speak with you. Fair day." The healer walked past Ryk and Elaine.

One quick look told Jehna what Ryk wanted. "Cousin." She

waited.

Ryk looked a bit uncomfortable. "You were right. I'd like to court Elaine."

"She's agreed?"

"Of course, I have," Elaine interjected.

"May the All Knowing One bless you both."

The pair went toward the kitchen and Jehna chuckled. Taken Ryk long enough. Now all she needed was to be officially recognized by the clan chiefs as a household and their leader. Once done, she could sanction braidings and make other decisions.

Part of her couldn't wait. Part of her was scared. Yet, she knew her Uncle Daniel would not have trained her for the position if he didn't believe her capable. She hoped the All Knowing One agreed.

Chapter 20

Daniel sat staring at the com, a scowl on his face. The other clan leaders, except the Wayas, still balked at officially recognizing the new clan let alone Jehna as the leader. Which reminded him they'd need a family name. He'd discuss that with his niece the next time he talked with her.

"Still not agreeing?" He glanced at his wife Taeia, greeting her with a warm smile as he shook his head.

"Stubborn fools," she scoffed, lightly resting her hand on his shoulder.

"They have good reason." Or so they thought. He disagreed.

"If you thought that, you would never have allowed Jehna to set up a new household."

"You're correct." He pulled her down on his lap, giving her a quick kiss. His hand rested on her stomach. "And how is our future child?"

"Sleeping." Her hand rested on his. "It is a girl."

Her knowing did not surprise him. Wise Women had the ability to know the sex of the child long before it was born.

"Does this please you?" she asked, her face anxious.

"Very much." He hadn't expected to have another after Mikhal had been born. Between Taeia's duties as both his spouse and Arvona, plus raising their son and the orphaned children, there hadn't been much time to think about having more of their own.

"Good." She kissed him.

The com flickered indicating an incoming message and he sighed, knowing he needed to answer.

"I'd better get off your lap." She rose and gave him a wink from the door.

He laughed and answered the com. "This is Daniel Talon."

"Daniel!" the leader of the T'Ganth clan greeted, his eyes bright. "I got a message from our cousins on Charon." He paused. "The messengers have arrived."

"What?" His heart beat with excitement. Finally! They'd been waiting for centuries.

He nodded. "One problem. The Arkon's soldiers are involved. They want the unwelcome Earthers removed from Charon."

"How did an Earth colony end up there?" From what he understood, the Earth ships were normally regulated to planets outside the Five Systems and Borders.

His fellow clan leader shook his head. "Who knows how the All Knowing One works."

From previous experience he knew that to be true. "Then we are blessed."

"I've contacted the other clans. Each of them are sending a ship to hopefully have a messenger to bring back to their Homefall." He hesitated before asking, "Anyone you can spare?"

Daniel did a quick inventory. Lonn Talu and Torey Gi'an were arranging a trade on Ladou, although what the vampires could possibly have to trade he wasn't certain. Mostly they kept to themselves, so to reach out to the Rovers concerned him. At least he knew the two cousins were well from their last communication.

The uncles had projects they needed to complete. Ryyk needed to overhaul his engines. His blood cousin Lon however, had been in port for a couple of days. He might enjoy a trip to Charon.

"Think I might have an available pilot."

"I'd get him to Charon as fast as possible. The Arkon's soldiers are not known for their patience."

~ * ~

Daniel found Lon in the garden enjoying the shade and trickling fountain. Twelve cycles older than his cousin, the younger man was more like a son. They shared the family facial features, while Lon had ebony hair streaked with a shock of white. Possibly something he'd inherited from his mother who had died giving him life.

"Hello, Lon," Daniel greeted, sitting down on the stone ledge.

"You have a run you need me to do."

"Perceptive as always," he complimented his cousin. "The messengers have arrived and I have need of a ship and a captain to bring them to our Homefall."

He watched the realization play over the younger man's face. "They're here?"

Daniel nodded.

"It would be my honor." Lon stood up. "Where are they?"

"Charon."

"How'd they'd get there?"

"No idea." Getting to his feet, Daniel clapped Lon's shoulder. "I am trusting you to bring them safely here."

Lon smiled a look of pride on his face. "Of course. I'll leave right away." He hurried away toward the landing field. The *Talon 9* would shortly be on its way.

"He wants to please you," Taeia said, as she joined him.

"Lon always has."

"I'm surprised you didn't send Mikhal." She sounded more curious than upset.

"He has a braiding to prepare for."

"Ah." She rested her head on his shoulder. "What bride price has Ryk asked for?"

"He has not yet named it." The wait concerned Daniel.

An orange and blue lizard flicked its tongue at Daniel before scuttling across the stones and finding a spot to lick up water. The creatures lived all over the compound and kept down the various pests.

"Does that concern you?" Taeia's question brought his mind back to his son's pending braiding ceremony.

"Not really. I suspect Ryk hadn't thought about it."

"They are braiding young."

"So did Mark and Gem." He lightly touched her face. "We weren't much older when we braided."

"At my sister's insistence." Her eyes still held sadness. "She was taken from us too soon."

And the Arkon had something belonging to the Talon clan, which Daniel had every intention of reclaiming. How, he wasn't sure. When the timing was right, the All Knowing One would make a way.

~ * ~

Daniel watched his spouse sleep, wrapped warmly in blankets. Although she was with child, no one in the Homefall knew yet. Soon he'd have to make the announcement. No doubt they'd be happy for him. The birth of a Rover child was always celebrated.

Through the partially open window he watched the wind move the leaves in a dance he knew well. Night could be nippy after the warmth of the day. They'd adjusted to change during their lives as had all those who had come before them.

Jehna had spoken of heavy rains and snow at the Saris Homefall. Ronia never experienced that kind of weather. On rare occasions the sky sent a drenching torrent refilling their lake, all the plants drinking deeply, growing at a surprising rate uncommon for their normal seasons.

Leaving the room he walked their home. Two bedrooms, a sitting area, his office and a small cooking area comprised the stone sided dwelling. A set of stairs went up and he climbed them, taking a seat in the open area. Silence greeted him.

When all the family were on Homefall often he'd find many wandering the grounds, talking, laughing, enjoying being together. With so many choosing to join Jehna, part of him worried they would not have enough pilots for trades. The older uncles had ships, yet they'd grounded themselves to work on projects to make their home stronger.

Large dark wings fluttered, setting on the edge overlooking below. Brilliant yellow eyes blinked at him, before the creature settled down, turning its attention to hunt for potential prey. The flyers had their uses with a head which appeared to turn all the way around. He knew they didn't. Puffy feathers covering their entire bodies, sharp claws for catching small prey and a haunting cry.

Its cry reminded him of a night fifteen cycles ago. One which he tried to push out of his mind and not think of. The honor had been his and he'd accepted it. Still a sense of loss filled him.

"Can't sleep?" He turned to face his life mate. She'd thrown a sylk over her shoulders, its soft fabric keeping her safe from the nippy air.

"Hoping we haven't lost too many."

Her keen green eyes looked at him as if to fathom the truth. "I have no doubt we have enough." She sat beside him on the bench. "Not often a flyer perches there."

"'Tis a rare occasion," he agreed.

"As Mikal's braided, Tuleh will be an excellent addition."

"Ryk trained her well." He knew the young woman would be a good helper for his son.

Quiet enveloped them. He put his arm around Taeia, enjoying being with her. Soon they'd have another baby in the house. Probably a grandchild as well, depending on how quickly his son and

Tuleh decided to start a family. Mikal already had established his own trades.

With a start Daniel realized he'd always intended to have Jehna succeed him as clan leader until he'd seen the need for a new Homefall. He wondered if his son would be interested in being trained to be their next leader.

"Lon would be a better choice," Taeia said softly as if she'd read his mind. "He has patience and wisdom." She smiled. "Not to mention following you and Jehna while you were training her."

"Huh." He'd never considered his blood cousin as a potential leader. When Lon got back, they'd have a long talk. "You see true."

"I see what needs to be seen." She shivered. "Come back to bed."

"Shortly."

She sighed, kissing his cheek and he listened to her steps as she descended the stairs.

The flyer turned its round head to stare at him once more. "You'd do me a great favor if you'd catch the little thief who keeps stealing some of our seed." Wings extended, the flyer swooped silently down, claws extended. He heard a shrill screech and knew the creature would feed well.

Rising, Daniel stared out, every building, tree, and burbling fountain familiar to him. He'd been born, raised and trained here to be clan chief. Soon the messengers would arrive. What change would they bring with them and would they become part of the family or would they leave to share with others.

With a heavy sigh he decided to rejoin Taeia. The All Knowing One had the matter well in hand. Him worrying about the future of the clan was needless.

Now, if he could just get the other leaders to accept Jehna and establish her as clan leader. With so many opposing it would be a hard-won battle. One he'd prepared well for.

~ * ~

His day always started just before the sun rose. Daniel sat in his office going over the figures for his Homefall. Ryk could ask any bride price he wished and it would be easy to accommodate. Question was, why hadn't his cousin?

Deciding he needed to speak with Jehna, he tuned the com.

Demtrie's smiling face welcomed him. "Greetings, Daniel Talon."

"Jehna about?"

"Been up early today." The older man turned and spoke, "Tanner, go tell Jehna her Uncle Daniel wishes to speak with her."

So, the wolf had been in the com tower. Still amazed him three Arial had chosen to be her companions. The older race rarely left their home world. How they'd come to join her, Jehna had never shared.

For a few minutes he visited with Demtrie discussing the current weather. Not a word about possible courtings or trades. Either the man didn't know, or he felt Daniel shouldn't hear the news from him.

Jehna appeared, taking the Wayas's place. "Thanks, Demtrie. Holly will be here shortly with your breakfast."

"My thanks." The older man withdrew so not to overhear.

"So Uncle," Jehna began. "What news?"

"The Messengers have arrived." He expected her to be surprised. She only nodded.

"We'd heard. Tamzin told us."

He chuckled. "She always seems to hear the news first."

"Part of her trade."

"I was contacted by the T'ganths. The messengers are coming to the Homefalls. I sent Lon."

"Good choice." She tilted her head. "He'd make a good clan leader."

"So Taeia informed me." Why didn't it surprise him, Jehna thought the same.

"He followed us around enough." She frowned. "You don't think Mikal would be."

"He enjoys the trade." He shifted. "Has Ryk decided on his bride price yet?"

"I'll speak with him."

"Thank you. Would you prefer the braiding ceremony be on Saris or Ronia."

"Ronia definitely. I'm sure Ryk and Tuleh will agree."

"How are things on at your Homefall?"

She smiled. "Ryk asked to court Elaine. Finally."

"Good. He needs to rebraid."

"I reminded him."

"And yourself?"

She glanced away. "There is someone coming who will stand at my side. I don't know them."

He started realizing what she meant. "Does Taeia know?"

"Not yet." Tanner put his muzzle on Jehna's leg. "I suspect it's time I go. We'll talk more as is needed."

"I'll let you know when the messengers arrive."

"Thank you, Uncle. Fair trade."

"Fair trade," he replied as he broke the connection. His eyes flickered over his desk even as his nose detected a spicy aroma. Taeia was making his favorite. With a smile he headed to their kitchen, knowing his duties could, for a short time, wait until later.

Chapter 21

Jehna found Ryk sitting at the table, a cup of cof in his hand. She sat across from him and waited to see if he noticed her.

"Cousin," he greeted. "You're up earlier than normal. Still dark."

"Had a few things I wanted to do before everyone rises."

Faint noises came from the kitchen. "Denebie's up. Probably Elaine too." He smiled referring to the woman he courted.

"Uncle Daniel wants to know if you've settled on a bride price yet."

He sipped his cof before answering. "I have an idea."

"How much is it going to cost him?"

"I'm thinking it will be a fair trade." He glanced up at her. "I'll contact him in a couple of days."

"Acceptable." Jehna didn't need to know. Bride price was his concern as Tuleh's father.

"What's the news?"

Roury bounced in and placed a cup of tea before Jehna. "Hi."

"Morning Roury. Helping in the kitchen?" she teased.

"Yep. Gotta go feed the kittens." He darted out.

"Errl is going to have his hands full," Ryk observed.

"I think he can handle it. As I recall, Mark, Aaron and Adrian were always into mischief."

"Errl was forced to grow up faster than he wanted."

"In some ways I think we all were."

"Don't disagree with you, cousin." He held his mug, his eyes holding a far-away look. "Even I hadn't expected to start building trades after purchasing my ship." Ryk took a swallow. "I expected my father," he stopped, a trace of old sorrow flickering over his face.

Jehna knew how he felt. "We all suffered loss." She considered her next words. "I still regret not getting the chance to know my father." Jehna wrapped her hands around her cup, allowing the warmth to chase the chill from her fingers. "My mother never talked much about him."

"What was it like living on Sharmain? You've never shared."

"Lots of training, learning various plants and how to grow or use them."

"Like my father did for me when I was maybe three or four cycles."

"My mother started my training at a younger age." She stared at her cup.

"You were maybe five cycles when you came to Ronia, if I remember."

"Ten." She corrected, glancing up as Hawk flew over, finding a high perch. Russet feathers fluffed before he preened his wings. Jehna watched briefly before answering. "I sometimes wonder if those of Arial regret leaving behind their true form."

"Maybe why would be the question," Ryk suggested.

"I don't think they'd tell me."

"Maybe they don't know."

She met her cousin's gaze. "Oh, they know. They've chosen not to share."

~ * ~

Two days later Ryk climbed the stone stairs to the com tower. Demtrie sat at a small table, his attention focused on this lunch. Denebie had made a thick stew and Elaine had added fluffy biscuits. The older man obviously enjoyed his food.

"You should join the family," Ryk suggested.

"Have all I need up here," he answered. "Holly comes up to visit as do others."

"Heard Forrest is coming home soon." Ryk glanced out the window. Every ship sat on the field. Many trades had been completed and they'd celebrated around the table sharing tales.

"Checked in this morning," Demtrie added, taking another bite.

"Good." Altair had been in a better mood and he'd heard her humming as she tended the plants, showing her daughter Arissa how to care for them.

"Besides, taking those stairs grate on my bones."

"You should talk to Altair."

"She's given me a couple of mixtures." He shrugged. "Easier to stay off my feet and rest."

Ryk nodded, knowing aging was not easy on everyone. "Need to use the com."

"Go ahead." Demtrie took another spoonful of stew.

Taking a deep breath, the Rover sat down, giving himself a moment before contacting his Uncle Daniel. Figuring out a bride price for his daughter proved to be far more difficult than he'd expected. Usually it was a credit amount, which the clan leader could easily pay. Yet thinking on it, Ryk knew while it would be useful, there were other needs as well.

Daniel's face appeared and he smiled at Ryk. "I'm guessing you've decided."

"I have." Ryk paused, forming his words carefully. "Part trade, part payment."

His uncle's face took on an interested expression nodding for the younger man to continue. Ryk gave him an amount. Daniel agreed. "What else did you have in mind?"

"Two Valqurie horses." The household would need them and Ryk knew it.

His uncle considered before replying, "Steep price."

"I know."

The clan chief pursed his lips, thinking. He turned his head and Ryk heard another voice in the background. "Consider it done," he finally replied. "When do you want to set the braiding for?"

"In another quarter cycle Tuleh turns fifteen." Seemed too young to him for her to braid, but she and Mikhal had grown up together. His daughter had assured him they wanted this.

"Mikhal came of age not long ago."

Ryk already knew. "I know we usually wait, but they've both agreed."

"Mikhal started his own trades at thirteen cycles, had his ship at fourteen."

"By your approval, as I remember." Ryk waited to see what the clan leader's response would be.

"He learned quickly." Daniel shook his head. "He's never left the Borders, which was his agreement with me."

Ryk had suspected there had been a condition. "How's Aunt Taeia?"

"She's well."

"Good to hear." Ryk leaned forward. "Fair trade."

"Fair trade," Daniel responded before cutting the transmission.

"Steep price," Demtrie commented.

"My daughter is worth it."

~ * ~

Ryk joined the others around the main table. The children had taken over one end, raptly paying attention to Errl as he shared a funny story. They laughed as he finished and he started when a silvery white cat landed on the table, sitting down as if the creature had every right to do so.

"Nice to see you're back, Crystal," Jehna greeted.

The Felcat blinked at her before washing her paw and rubbing the side of her face with it.

"Wherever do they vanish to?" Denebie asked from her place beside Errl.

"No idea," Gem answered, taking a drink of cocacof. "They vanish for a while and then return."

"I doubt they'll ever say," Jehna added. "My impression is they go home for some sort of important event and when it's over they return. Beyond that…" she shrugged.

"You live strangely here." Denebie reached out to pet the cat, who moved away and sauntered down the table.

"I should tell you to get down." Jehna offered a hand, which Crystal sniffed before deigning to allow a pet. "I'm glad you're back. You were missed."

"They always are," Ryk agreed. Elaine poured him cof and set a plate in front of him.

"Bride price settled?" Jehna glanced at him.

He nodded. "Settled." The cof was hot and he savored the bitter flavor.

"Still think it's wrong," Elaine huffed.

"Tradition," the rest of the family answered.

Elaine looked startled. "Oh." Her cheeks turned a charming shade of pink. Ryk reached up and gently touched her face.

Various conversations started up. Mark, Gem and Aaron needed to do some maintenance of their ships. Adrian and Shala had moved to the fireplace, exchanging longing glances. Ryk suspected there might soon be a baby conceived. Jehna sipped her tea, her eyes distant. Holly paced to the door as if expecting someone to arrive.

"Forrest will get home when he arrives," Ryk reminded her, pushing his now empty plate away.

"I know."

Altair wiped her cheeks. "Arissa come. We have plants to attend."

Her daughter sighed, leaving the other children as Errl launched into another story. "I want to listen."

"Later," her mother promised as they left.

"I remember those days," Jehna commented. "Lots of learning and rarely time to play."

"You're also a wise woman." Elaine finally sat next to Ryk.

"Aunt Taeia completed my training, even while Uncle Daniel prepared me to become a clan leader." She took another sip. "We'll need a clan name."

"We're a mix." Ryk glanced around the room. Wellers, Talons, Wayas, Colons and others. "Any ideas cousin?"

"Not yet." She traced patterns on the table. "We can think on it while the clan leaders make up their minds."

Denebie spoke. "You seem quite young to be a clan leader."

"Uncle Daniel was seventeen cycles. I'm older than he was." Jehna sipped her tea. Crystal jumped off the table and padded over to the fireplace her head turned upward, her tail swishing back and forth.

"The disease that swept through," Errl explained, "caused the deaths of our parents and older Rovers."

"Yet some of you survived." Denebie placed her hand on Errl's.

"We did," he agreed. "I'm not sure how we survived those first days."

"Because we had to," Ryk reminded him. "Those of us who were older knew what to do."

"And Uncle Daniel had been trained," Jehna added. "He knew how to direct us."

"I heard some dark rumors on Aris," Elaine told them. "That the Nobles had a hand in it."

"I don't see how." Ryk narrowed his eyes.

"All I know is they are jealous of the Rovers controlling the trade routes." Elaine gathered up Ryk's plate. "I doubt that has changed."

Chapter 22

Daniel hurried into their bedroom where his life mate rested. "Lon just checked in and will be landing shortly."

"He has the messengers?" Taeia stretched, before her hand touched where their child grew.

"How is our daughter?"

"Fine." She put on light shoes. "I wonder if we should have a celebration."

"After being on the ship for several days, I think they'd like time to rest and get used to their new home." He held Taeia in his arms giving her a light kiss.

"We've waited so long."

"We can wait a bit longer."

Together they walked to the main gate as Lon walked across the sand with three men and three women, along with a young girl and an infant.

"More children." Taeia sounded delighted.

He noticed the other Felcats running to greet the visitors. An orange-colored cat strolled out and bumped noses with the others.

"Felcat," he observed.

"They act like they haven't seen each other for a long time."

"Perhaps they haven't."

The Felcats moved past them, going under the trees. Daniel looked over the messengers. His eyes settled on a man who walked with an air of assurance and command. He wore some sort of dark green splotched uniform and he assumed the man was a soldier, like the younger man who wore similar attire.

"The messengers," Lon introduced, sweeping his hand to indicate the group. "They speak the Earth language."

Switching from Rici, normally spoken by all Rovers, he tackled the Earth language. Jehna had more practice and he almost wished she were present.

"This is Daniel Talon," Lon introduced him. "And the Arvona Taeia. They're braided."

The older man stepped forward, his hand raising slightly before he lowered it. "I'm Major Lawrence Henry." He indicated each person as he introduced them. "My sister Dr. Susanna Gates. Her daughter Geri." The man indicated the baby she carried. "Her fiancé Kal Devon and his niece Krissy." The little girl hid behind her uncle gazing at Daniel shyly. "My younger sister Jeanie and this is Corporal Jack Lewis." He turned to the woman standing beside him, gave her a smile. "Dr. Amira Upala."

"And that orange cat is Leli," Jeanie informed them. "He sure seems friendly with all your cats."

"Felcats," Daniel corrected her. She started to ask another question and he raised his hand. "We'll answer all your questions at another time. I'm sure you're tired after your long journey. Taeia, please show the messengers to their quarters."

"Of course. If you'll follow me." She led the group away.

"Sorry I couldn't give you more notice." Lon shifted from one foot to the other. "The Arkon's soldiers wanted them gone."

"And the other clans?"

"Also transported messengers to their Homefalls." His blood cousin looked at him. "I can't believe they're finally here."

Nor could he. "Any idea how they ended up on Charon?"

"Not for certain. One of the messengers stayed behind and soldiers took the colony leader to Aris."

"And the rest?"

"Relocated."

"Do you know where?"

"As usual, that is information they decided we didn't need to know."

"Thank you, Lon." Daniel turned to head back onto the main grounds. "After you've eaten, I'd like to speak with you."

"Of course, Uncle." Lon hurried away. The younger man loved the gardens and would spend some time there before the evening meal.

As he passed the gate Daniel silently thanked the All Knowing One for keeping his promise.

~ * ~

The main hall seemed empty to Daniel with so many of their clan having decided to join the new household on Saris. Not that their number would be small for long. Mikhal would be braiding soon and he hoped his blood cousin Lon would find a woman. As for Lonn Talu and Torey Gi'an he couldn't be sure. The two young men had been looking around, but not found anyone they were interested in.

He glanced up. Both Uncles Jeremy and Assar entered, taking their normal places. They inclined their heads at Daniel continuing whatever discussion they'd started. Not unusual as the two oldest members of the clan.

Lon entered escorting their guests and waved them to a seat at the table. Lawrence, if Daniel remembered correctly, glanced at the other tables and at the only one that was occupied.

"We were told the Talon clan is the largest." He sat down across from Daniel, the others taking places on either side of the soldier. He still wore his uniform.

"We are," Daniel confirmed, smiling at his wife as she worked to set up the buffet. Lonn and Torey had assisted her as they had with the cooking. They both grinned when they finished taking a place next to Lon. Ryyk joined them too.

"Where's everyone else?" Lawrence inquired.

"We're setting up a second Homefall," Daniel explained. "Many decided to join it."

"From what I understand," the soldier continued, "I thought the clans had lived on the same planets for a long time."

"Correct. Two clans became so small they merged. That would be the V'ianths and T'ganths. That happened," he looked at his wife who joined him.

"Before any of us were born." She poured his favorite wine and handed him the glass. He smiled his thanks.

"We met the T'ganths." Susanna shifted her baby, who slept. "They never told us they'd merged with another clan."

"Healthy child." Daniel glanced at Taeia and she gave him a sweet smile.

"You can help yourselves to the food." She gestured toward the food laid out on a side table.

"You have enough to feed an army." Lawrence grinned.

"At times it has felt that way." She sipped her favorite juice, made from a small orange fruit she raised in her private garden.

"Are you the only woman here?" the female doctor asked.

"For the moment."

"My son will be braiding with Tuleh Sargol in a quarter cycle."

He glanced up as Mikhal took his place next to his father. "We've known each other all our lives," he added. "We always knew we'd braid, just like Mark and Gem did."

"How old are you?" Lawrence asked.

"I'm of age."

"You look like a teenager."

The young man frowned. "I'm fifteen cycles and have been trading since I was thirteen, had my own ship at fourteen."

With a surprised look the messenger stared at Daniel. "And you're fine with him...braiding?" He frowned. "What is braiding?"

"A couple pledge their lives together," Mikhal explained.

"I think he means marriage, Larry." Susanna gave Kal a smile. "Like we intend to."

"Is he the father of your child?" Daniel didn't want to pry, he was curious.

"No. My husband died in an accident. Geri was born after, at our colony." Her eyes met Daniel's. "Any idea what happened to the rest of the colonists?"

He shook his head. "Difficult to say where the Arkon had them relocated."

"Any idea where Leli is?" The younger woman glanced around.

"The Felcats," Taeia explained, "live with us because we accept them for who they are. I have no doubt they are hunting or perhaps enjoying the cool of the evening."

"They are loyal," Mikhal added, "to those they have chosen. Leli will return to you."

"He'd better. Jack," she turned to the young soldier. "Let's get some food."

"We thank the All the Knowing One first." Daniel watched them.

"Prayer. Who would have thought huh, big brother?" Jeanie grinned.

He gave her a loving, reproachful look. "We're here for a reason, as you both should well know."

Daniel spoke, "We thank you for our food and for the messengers you promised and who have finally arrived. In praise." He pointed at the buffet. "Please help yourselves."

Everyone rose, filled their plates, cups or glasses. Daniel listened to the various conversations around the table. Talk of upgrades to their fueling system, suggestions on how to overhaul engines, and Taeia sharing tips on raising a baby with Susanna. Krissy stayed close to her uncle, although her eyes kept closing.

He remembered the children he'd raised being the same way. Tired, fighting it, as if they'd miss something.

"We have much to learn about each other." Larry took a swig of cof, his meal eaten. "That was very good," he complimented Taeia.

"I had help." She pointed at the young men.

Daniel agreed. "There is much to share and we will not learn it all tonight."

"I'm curious." Larry tapped the edge of his cup. "How long has this prophecy been around about the messengers."

Daniel shook his head. "We aren't sure. Many generations."

"Huh." He smiled at his sister. "It's been a long day. Why don't you turn in."

"I think I will." Susanna shifted the sleeping baby as she got to her feet.

"Can you find your way?" Taeia half rose.

"We'll be fine. Thank you."

Kal lifted the little girl and the pair left.

"Will we meet the rest of your clan?" Lawrence's question brought Daniel's attention back to him. Jeanie and Jack had wandered down and joined the four young men. They all eyed the young woman and he smiled as the soldier put his arm around her.

"Probably at the braiding ceremony."

"I'm going to say good night." Amira stifled a yawn.

"Sweet dreams." Lawrence smiled at her.

"You too."

They were a couple or they were trying to be. Why did Daniel sense an imbalance? Taeia's expression seemed to echo his thought.

"I like to be called Larry," the soldier shared.

"I'll remember that."

Chapter 23

Bugling echoed over the landing field and Ryk shaded his eyes as a large figure flew over, before settling next to the ships. A human figure slid off the dragon's back and a large feline jumped, its muscles taking the impact with ease.

Forrest grinned as he trotted over, his eyes glancing over the cats who played around the barn. "Where's Jehna?"

"Com tower. Clan leader meeting. Uncle Daniel wanted her to attend." Ryk motioned for Roury to stay away from the dragon. "What did the Shellmaster find?"

"Mostly documents and other records of those who first settled there." Forrest frowned. "The Shellmaster was a bit secretive. Told me he needed to study his findings before he shared."

The dragon spread out his wings and settled closer to the ground. The feline tucked under one of the wings.

"Didn't sleep last night," Forrest explained. "Too excited."

Took a lot for them to get excited and not sleep as Ryk recalled. "We'll let them nap." He raised his voice. "Roury, would you help me brush down the horses?"

The boy looked disappointed, his gaze fixed on the dragon. "Okay," he conceded.

"You need a bath," Ryk told Forrest, "which I suggest you take before you see Altair."

"Good idea. I smell like dragon." His cousin hurried toward the main house.

Ryk chuckled. He smelled of more than that. Going back in the barn, he fed the horses, brushed them down, with the boy's help and then watched as Roury played with the kittens. They were growing quickly and had learned from their mother how to deal with various pests.

Hawk stirred in the rafters swooping down and settling on the stall's top board. The bird cocked his head watching the kittens and the boy interact.

"I know you only talk to Jehna." Ryk kept a respectful distance. "But sure would like to know what your thoughts are right now."

Turning his head, Hawk looked at him. Intelligence flickered in the black eyes before he took flight out the open door.

"Good hunting," he called after the bird.

~ * ~

"We have a good-sized start for a new clan," Jehna informed the clan council, her image hovering over the com. "More than we expected plus local allies."

The men shifted almost as if they were uneasy. She suspected they hadn't expected the Homefall to get established so quickly.

"You've led well," the Wayas leader Cameron agreed. "Demtrie speaks well of you."

Andron Jovan frowned. "Hasn't this diminished the size of the Talon clan?" he asked Daniel.

"I have several young men who are seeking brides. Won't be long before we increase in size again."

Digon V'ianeth tapped his fingers. "Unusual for a woman to be a clan leader."

"But not unheard of," Daniel interjected. "According to our own history, many of the braided took over when they lost their life mate. Male and female."

A murmuring echoed over the com. Jehna hid her smile. Her Uncle was correct.

"She's also a Wise Woman," the T'ganth leader objected.

"My household has a fully trained Wise Woman." Jehna gave them a stern look. "She's being courted." Jehna watched the other leader's expressions. Andron was surprised, as were the others, except her uncle who already knew.

"That's good," the Jovan leader reluctantly agreed, although she suspected it cost him. "Who's courting her?"

There'd be no harm in telling him. "Forrest Wayas."

~ * ~

After the meeting concluded, she and her uncle had a quick discussion. Daniel wanted to know her thoughts and she'd been honest with him. He'd also given her a special piece of personal news.

"Taeia is pregnant. The child is a girl."

"You must be thrilled." Her aunt was older, but not too old to have another child or two.

"I am." He'd grinned. "It'll be nice to have a baby in the house."

"What does Mikhal think?"

"We haven't told him yet."

"You probably should. When will you tell the rest of the clan?"

"At the braiding feast."

Jehna had another question she wanted to ask, yet knew the time was not yet.

"You and the others will attend?" Daniel sounded doubtful.

"Of course, we will." She sat back in the chair. "Do you think we'd miss seeing Tuleh braided?"

"Good." His face held a baffled expression. "The Messengers are not what I thought they'd be."

"Meaning they aren't mystical beings." She'd heard the same stories growing up.

He looked relieved she understood. "They're likable enough."

"I can't wait to meet them." She'd stretched. "Forrest got home today." Jehna had seen the dragon land. "I need to find out what the Shellmaster found."

"Our agreement with them has been long standing."

"For which I'm grateful."

"We all are. Fair trade, Cousin."

"Fair trade, Uncle." They ended their communication and she joined the others.

Denebie and Elaine were working on the midday meal. Altair and Forrest, his hair still damp, stood next to the indoor fountain talking, Arissa standing by her mother. No doubt there would be an adoption there when the pair braided. Jehna had not asked about the child's father and would wait to see if the healer ever volunteered the information.

"They're well matched." Ryk pointed his chin in the pair's direction.

"They are indeed," she agreed. Errl and Roury were placing plates, glasses and cups on the table. The young boy smiled at the older man with admiration. She wondered if Denebie and her cousin would have more children.

"Where's Tanner and Dannon?"

"Hunting," she answered Ryk's question. "They'll be back in a day or two."

"You never worry?"

"No." She never did. They'd been together for almost ten cycles. She'd learned to trust them.

~ * ~

Harrison turned the horses out into the pasture. For the past eight days the temperatures had slowly warmed and the ground was thawed and dry enough to allow them some freedom to run. He smiled watching them gallop across the enclosure calling to each other. One of the dogs was lying just inside the fence where he could keep a watch on the horses.

The other dogs barking drew his attention and he hurried out of the barn. Riding in from the Rover neighbors was a woman he'd bet was the Argollian healer. They stopped in front of the house and the man dismounted. He smiled at Harrison. "Forrest Wayas."

The dogs sniffed him, but stayed away from his companion.

"Harrison Talbot," he returned as the woman tossed back her hood. She had blonde hair carefully pulled back in a braid.

"Altair Dawne," she introduced herself. "From what I understand, your wife is with child."

"She is."

"I would like to attend her. Make certain all is well with them both."

He smiled. "Thank you. I'd appreciate that. Door is open."

She inclined her head and went inside.

"Long ride for a visit." Harrison waited for the Rover to answer.

"Children are worth any price."

Seeing no threat from the visitors, the dogs took off after a grounder trying to sneak past. The chubby rodent ran and would probably escape without being caught.

"Horses could use some water, if you wouldn't mind."

"Bring them to the barn." He led the way and helped draw water for the animals. "Haven't heard anything thing from your leader."

"Stormy weather." Forrest rubbed his horse's neck. "Not much going on really."

He crossed his arms over his chest, wincing slightly. One of the cows had kicked him and he still hadn't healed.

"Should have Altair look at your injury before we leave."

"Thought she was here to take care of my wife."

"Healers take care of everyone." Forrest smiled. "I see the cats have been busy."

"Yeah. Do a great job of keeping the barn free of pests and mom cat took them hunting in the seed shed." The feline and her family had made short work of the few rodents there.

"Glad they worked out."

"Where did your cousin manage to find cats and dogs? They're rare here."

With a shrug he replied, "I don't know. The Wellers have contacts most of us don't."

"Huh. Heard there's a Shellmaster visiting."

"Got back a few days ago."

"Find anything interesting?" He'd intended to visit the ruins, yet never had the time. Harrison didn't regret selling them to Jehna Talon.

"Not sure." Forrest walked to the other door and watched the horses frolic.

"Your cousin took good care of them." The trade for two horses still seemed a bit steep, but then, Ryk Sargol had gone to get them. "His daughter is good with animals."

"At one time," the Rover answered.

He wanted to ask more questions, yet sensed they wouldn't be answered. Maybe one day he'd ask the captain directly. "He's a few orbits older than Jehna."

Forrest nodded.

"You're a man of few words."

Blue eyes darted his way. "I talk when I need to."

"Understood. How about cup of cof?"

"Sounds good."

They left the barn and entered the house. Molly hurried around setting the table. Forrest started to object and she interrupted him. "You'll not leave here with an empty stomach."

"She always like that?" Forrest asked.

"Yeah." He pulled off his coat and tossed it on a hook. Forrest pulled off his cloak, placing it next to the healers.

The two men shared a comfortable silence before the fire as its warmth filled the room. A short time later his wife and the healer came out of the bedroom.

"Your wife is fine and the baby healthy," she told him.

"Glad to hear it." He grinned at his wife. She blushed.

"I should be back in thirty days or so, to check again. If you have need please send a message."

"Thank you, I will."

"Lunch is ready," Molly announced as she placed a hearty stew and hot biscuits on the table.

The scent of beef reached his nose and his stomach growled. He'd eaten breakfast just before sunrise. He motioned to the table. "Please join us."

The healer started to say something and Forrest shook his head.

"That is most kind." She put her bag with her cloak.

Harrison escorted his wife to the table and their guests joined them. The two women chatted, Lissa asking questions about raising a baby, which the healer answered. He listened hoping to learn more. Not having been around children, he knew he had lots to learn.

After they ate, the Rover and healer took their leave and he watched them ride away. The dogs started to follow and he whistled. After a few moments the dogs trotted back.

"I've got work to finish," he called to his wife who stood in the door. "We'll talk later."

"Look forward to it." Lissa went back inside.

"Come on," he said to the dogs.

With a final look at the horses, he grabbed a shovel. Time to muck out the barn.

Time with his wife, no matter how much he wanted to forget the chores for once, would have to wait until later. He wished the Rover had been talkative. How were they doing with their new Homefall? Not that he really needed to know. Maybe when it got warmer he'd go find out for himself.

And what had the dragon found?

Chapter 24

Ryk nodded at Forrest as he brought the horses in and started taking off the saddles. Dark had just fallen and he'd been wondering if the two would opt to stay at the ranch and return in the morning. The other two horses whinnied a greeting. "How was your ride?"

"Fine." He carried the gear back to the tack room and started rubbing down the horses. "Mind if I give them some oats? They've earned it."

"You don't have to ask."

"Habit."

"Forrest." The younger man stopped and looked at him. "You're part of this clan now."

"Clan without a name."

"Won't have a name until Jehna is recognized by the other leaders." Ryk frowned. Maybe he should talk to Jehna about that.

The other man grunted. "See the Shellmaster is still here."

"You know them, they're never in a hurry."

Forrest laughed.

"You and Altair have time to talk."

"Some. She wanted to know if I'd adopt Arissa."

"That's your right."

"I know."

"I'll get water," Ryk offered.

"Thanks."

They'd found the well for the barn after the snows melted, or mostly melted, he reminded himself, dropping the bucket and pulling it up filled with fresh water. He carried it into the barn and filled the troughs for the horses.

Hawk swooped down catching a mouse and returned to the rafters.

"Good hunter." Forrest eyed the large predator.

"He is."

"How'd she end up with three male Arials?"

"No idea." The only story she'd never shared. "They came back with her after her second trade." He hung the bucket on a nail. "She may have told Uncle Daniel and Aunt Taeia." Maybe. Wasn't even sure she had. "They're accepted as part of the clan."

"And this one." Forrest tossed a blanket over each of the horses. "Dinner be waiting?"

Ryk chuckled. "Isn't it always?"

~ * ~

Noise filled the room as Ryk entered, Forrest darting to take a place next to Altair. Out of habit he sat at one end, with Jehna on the other. Bowls filled with bread, fruit, some vegetables and a platter of meat waited for them. Hot cof steamed from cups and coca for the children.

Jehna spoke, "To the All Knowing One our thanks for this bounty. In praise."

"In praise," everyone echoed.

Altair frowned and looked as if she wished to speak. Forrest squeezed her hand and she nodded, dropping her eyes to her empty plate.

Forrest and Altair shared a private discussion, Arissa looking bored casting longing looks at the other children. He wondered if she ever got to play or if her mother filled all her time with training.

When the meal ended, the children hurried to find a place near the fireplace, waiting for Errl to tell them stories. He rose, but Jehna shook her head. With a nod he sat down.

"Your story will need to wait a few metras," Jehna told them. "We have a matter of importance to discuss."

With a groan, the children sagged. "Boring adult stuff," one of them said.

"Boring adult stuff," Errl agreed. "Why don't you play a game while we talk."

They nodded and argued about which game to play.

Ryk sipped his cof and waited to see what Jehna wished to talk about.

"Uncle Daniel reminded me," she spoke without any introduction. "That our clan will need a name."

Silence followed. Ryk wondered if anyone had thought about it or had and waited for the right time to speak.

"It shouldn't carry any of our names." Holly lifted her cup, taking a sip.

"I agree with my sister." Forrest glanced at Ryk silently asking a question.

"Do you have an idea, cousin?" Ryk asked, settling his arms on the table, his eyes resting on Jehna.

"Possibly." Her eyes looked around the table. "I want to know if anyone else had a preferred name."

Mark and Gem exchanged a silent conversation. He remembered being able to do that with Mirra. Hopefully, in time, he and Elaine would share the same.

"You can't still be the Talon clan?" Denebie seemed confused.

"Talon's already are a clan," Jehna answered.

"As are the Wayas," Forrest added.

Adrian and Shala listened as did Aaron. They rarely spoke unless needed.

"Obvious name, Cousin," Errl tossed in, "would be to call us the Saris clan."

Elaine leaned toward Ryk. "Is he joking?"

Ryk shook his head, waiting to see Jehna's reaction.

She sipped her tea as if considering the suggestion. "It's not up to me." Placing her cup back on the table, she tapped her finger. "We'll leave a voting bowl. Black stone for no, a white one for yes or a written suggestion." Jehan pointed at the mantle. "We'll leave it there for three days and then tally."

A voting bowl! Ryk couldn't remember the last time one had been used. "Wise choice."

Everyone around the table nodded. "I will place it there, along with the stones, in the morning."

"We done?" Errl grinned.

His cousin sighed. "We're done."

"Good." Errl got up and the children stopped their argument and expectantly waited for their story.

Denebie shook her head. "They're getting spoiled."

"Welcome to the Rover life," Jehna responded with a smile.

~ * ~

Before dawn, Jehna set up the voting bowl, with two others filled with black and white stones. Writing material and an implement also waited in the event anyone wished to make a suggestion.

Entering the kitchen she discovered both Denebie and Elaine up, warming a pan of hot cereal along with pots of cof and coca. Several bowls were set out along with some covered dishes.

"You're both up early," she commented as she made her tea with her favorite blend. Her mother had taught her how to make it.

"I trust you slept." Denebie sounded accusing. "You have a habit of staying up all night."

"On rare occasions and as needed."

Elaine opened the oven and shoved in a pan full of coca pastry. "What do you think the outcome of the vote will be?"

"No idea." She sipped her tea. "I'll be in my office. Once breakfast is ready, I'd appreciate a tray."

"Of course," Denebie answered.

"Thank you."

Going back to her room and into her office, she sat down and stared at the work she had to do. With everyone in port, they could complete the last of the planting. She remembered doing the same on Ronia both as a child and an adult. A task she enjoyed along with her private garden of herbs.

After breakfast she'd need to hand out assignments. The sooner they planted, the faster they'd be able to harvest when it was time. Hopefully before the cold weather set in again.

Tanner wandered in, taking a whiff as the wind blew in some scent. 'Hunt?'

'If you like.'

Dannon, who dozed by the fireplace in her room, grumbled about the noise before falling silent.

'Up all night.' Tanner sounded amused.

'Hunted with the Shellmaster's companion. An honorable task.' Dannon grumped.

Tanner woofed and she listened to his nails click on the floor as he left. Jehna shook her head. Sometimes the pair were the best of friends and at other times, friendly rivals. Hawk tended to wait out the disagreements.

Speaking of her winged companion, he preferred to stay out in the barn and hunt when he liked. He watched over the cats and their young. They hadn't seen any sky predators, but that didn't mean with the warmer weather there weren't any. They had much to learn about this world.

"Morning." A light knock and Tuleh entered carrying a tray. She glanced at the desk as if asking where should she put it.

"I have a table in my room. Please put my tray there."

"Of course." The young woman left and she heard the door close quietly when Tuleh left.

With a shake of her head, Jehna knew she needed food before she could complete her tasks for the day. Going into her room, she gave a quick thanks before eating her thick hot cereal and munching on berries. A warm pot of tea had been sent as well. She'd have to thank the women in the kitchen later for their thoughtfulness.

When finished she poured herself another cup and retreated to her office. Her task would take all morning. Granted, she might have to shuffle tasks around if trades had been arranged. Still there was much to finish at Homefall.

~ * ~

After three days passed, she and Ryk gathered up the voting bowl and retreated to her office. Much to both their surprise, every stone in the bowl was white. No suggestions. No nos.

"For once Errl had a good idea," Ryk joked.

"We all know he's smarter than we give him credit for."

"When are you going to tell Uncle Daniel?"

"At Mikhail's and Tuleh's braiding."

"Think we'll get to meet the messengers?" Ryk's expression showed his hope.

Again a vision flashed before her eyes. A man she did not know stood beside her as ships filled their landing field. A sense of danger filled her and she took a deep breath as her eyes cleared.

"Cousin?"

"True sight comes when it comes." She shook her head as she sat down.

"Aaron ask yet to court Holly?"

"Aaron is not going to court her." Her eyes met her cousins. "Holly would like him to, but Aaron isn't ready to braid yet."

"He's spoken to you."

"No. I have only to watch him. He tolerates her sitting beside him. Never has he shown an interest."

"Holly will need to look for another."

"She'll find someone."

"No doubt." He paused. "When will you share the vote?"

"Tomorrow at breakfast. T'will be the best time."

~ * ~

Up again before the sun, Jehna stared out into the silent darkness. Wind whispered inside carrying with it scents of flowers she did not know. The trees around the hold had begun to bloom filling the courtyards with blue, lavender, yellow, red, and orange flowers and bright green vines hugged the rock. A couple contained white blooms with pale brown middles.

'Pretty.' Dannon brushed against her. Her fingers lightly pet his smooth head.

'Agreed.'

'Shellmaster very excited.'

'About his discovery?'

'Yes.' The leopard licked a spot on his shoulder. 'Not share why.'

'No doubt in time we'll know.' She still had no idea how long the dragon intended to stay.

Dannon placed both paws on the thin ledge so he could smell outside. 'Going out.' He landed quietly on the floor and padded out. The Arial had lived in the wilds of their planet for centuries. The Shellmasters had explored the abandoned cities and wondered why the decision had been made to leave them. Their technical accomplishments alone told of their ingenuity and talent. What could possibly have happened to make them wish to live in their animal forms?

Shaking her head Jehna smoothed the long skirt she rarely wore. With announcing the outcome of the vote, it seemed appropriate. Her Aunt Taeia had instilled some respect for tradition. Leaving her room she went below finding some family members already up. Ryk gave her a smile, while Errl held his mug and sipped his cof. He looked half asleep. Bowls of fruit and breads had already been laid out.

"Morning Jehna," Elaine greeted, putting a pot in front of her and a cup. "Everyone else should be down presently."

"How's the planting going?" she asked Ryk while she mixed her tea.

"Grains should be done in a few days. Thanks to Elaine's training, the orchards are in place." He chuckled. "She'll probably make more suggestions."

"They'll be welcome." She wondered what others the woman would make.

Laughter exploded as the children raced to find spots at the table. Gem poured coca for hers, filling two more cups for Arissa and Roury. Altair joined her daughter, her eyes darting to the entryway as Forrest and Holly joined them. Soon the table filled with members of the new clan—her clan—she reminded herself.

Ryk thanked the All Knowing One for their meal and the day before them. Eyes constantly looked in her direction, waiting for the announcement about their clan name. She ate her food, knowing they would have their answer soon enough.

"You ever going to tell us, Cousin?" Errl prodded, mischief dancing in his brown eyes.

"I wanted to wait until everyone finished." She took a sip of tea.

"It's the one thing we all want to know, cousin." He winked at her causing Denebie to frown at him.

Everyone, even the children, gazed at her.

Jehna took a breath. "We'll be called the Saris clan."

Shouting and cheers broke loose as everyone celebrated. "Here's to the Saris clan!" Errl raised his mug. "May we drink to it!"

Everyone followed his gesture and took a drink from their mugs.

"Too bad we can't celebrate," Denebie said.

"After Jehna is recognized as clan chief," Ryk reminded everyone. "We can celebrate then."

The one obstacle still in their way. She asked the All Knowing One to change the clan chiefs' minds and hearts almost every day. Always in timing not of her own making she'd been reminded.

"We all have work to do." Ryk rose to his feet. "Tuleh, you have a braiding to get ready for." His daughter smiled, a faint blush on her cheeks. "You're excused for the day."

"Thank you, Father."

He smiled fondly at his daughter. "Elaine, if you'd run the orchard crew with the finishing touches. Gem, the planters."

Both women nodded.

"Everyone else finish breakfast and then put your dishes in the sink." Ryk picked up his. "We have much to do."

Chapter 25

Daniel gazed out at his home. A hot breeze fluttered through, stirring the tree branches. A couple of lizards skittered across the ground, scurrying up the rocks and disappearing into the foliage. Much the same as it had been since he was a child. The only difference, the arrival of the messengers.

"Did they share anything of value?" Taeia asked, slipping her arm around him.

"They have much to teach us." He pulled her close giving her a kiss.

"They are not what you expected." She rested her hand against his chest.

"Too many stories and legends." Had he really expected them to be powerful all-knowing beings? Perhaps a secret part of him had. In truth, it was better they were mortal, making it easier to relate to them.

"I've heard them." Her eyes followed a man as he gazed at the trees, his green uniform almost helping him blend into the scenery. "Now would be a good time to speak with him."

A smile tugged at his lips. Taeia astute as always and wise. "Your sister teach you that?"

She gazed at him innocently. "What?"

"To always see what I cannot."

With a laugh she shook her head and pulled away. "You did."

Not sure if he believed her, he moved to join the man who gazed with interest at one of the lizards. Its orange and blue body rested on the stone as the sun touched the reptile's skin.

"What are they called?" his guest Larry asked.

"We've never named them. They keep away some of the pests so we encourage them to dwell among us."

"Interesting." He glanced around no doubt seeing the work being done for Mikhail's braiding. "When does your son's bride arrive?"

"Soon. She's not quite yet of age."

"Fifteen seems too young to marry."

"It happens rarely. Gem Morran and Mark Weller were an exception." He paused. "They always knew they'd braid."

"Huh." The man rubbed his jaw as if considering the idea.

"We are trained from a young age to trade and fly ships." Daniel pointed at a bench. The messenger nodded and sat down. Daniel joined him.

"You're forced to grow up fast."

"Rovers have been so from the beginning." Not the dark origins few knew about let alone shared.

"Your people do all the trading."

"We do." He watched the body language of the man. Relaxed, yet poised to fight if needed. "Others have specialized knowledge." The Simeons on two planets and the Wise Women on Sharmain. The dragons and the Felcats.

Speaking of which, Tam, a gray beauty with striking blue eyes joined him, sitting on the stone behind him, cleaning herself. Normally she stayed aboard his ship the *Talon 3*.

"Cat intelligent?"

"Felcat," he corrected, "and yes."

Larry threw a look he couldn't read at the feline. "How many from your clan joined the new…Homefall. That's what you call them correct?"

"You are correct," Daniel agreed. "More than expected."

"Does it hurt your household?"

Daniel shook his head. "Tuleh will braid with my son and join him here. There are others who are searching and no doubt will find brides. There is no hurry." He knew they had enough trades to keep the Homefall going for a long while.

"What happens at a braiding?"

"There is a brief ceremony and then a feast to celebrate." He smiled. "Many from Saris will be here as well."

"I heard you trained the woman who will be leading them."

"My cousin Jehna." He'd meant for her to take over the Talon Homefall, but starting a new one had been pressed upon him during a dream.

"Will your son take your place one day?"

"That's not his desire." He needed to speak to Lon and finish his training. The younger man had followed him and Jehna around cycles ago. Daniel decided it was time to ask a question. "Two of your party are ready to braid. It would not be unusual for there to be more than one ceremony."

Larry gave him a startled look. "You mean my sister Susanna and Kal."

Daniel nodded.

"They only recently became engaged. I'm not sure when they wanted to get married."

"And your younger sister and her soldier?"

The older soldier chuckled. "Jeanie and Jack like each other. As for marriage—" He shook his head. "I doubt the conversation has come up."

"My impression is that they are well matched."

"Yeah, maybe. We'll see."

"What about yourself?" Daniel hadn't yet figured out why their match seemed wrong.

"I don't know. Amira…" He stopped as if sharing were more than he could bear. "There's no hurry." Larry rose. "What do you do all day?"

"Depends on the day." Daniel got to his feet. "Today I need to visit the uncles and see if their projects are going well."

"The two older men I saw at dinner."

"Yes."

"May I ask one question?"

"I do not guarantee to answer."

"Fair enough. I noticed the uncles were the only older people here. Where are the others?"

Daniel felt a tightness in his chest. "They're dead."

"I'm sorry." The man paused. "Mind if I ask how that happened? You don't have to tell me if you don't want to." His tone was kind.

"You'll find out eventually. Walk with me."

The other man matched his pace as he headed across the grounds. They passed a few others who inclined their heads. He stopped when he reached the Memory Wall, on the far side of the grounds. On each stone a name had been carved. His hand rested on two. "My parents."

Larry looked at them frowning. "At another time I'll ask how you honor your dead."

The curved structure expanded back as far as the eye could see, with smaller similar structures inside. All the clan leaders were represented along the wall near the lake.

"You asked what happened." Daniel steeled himself. Few outside the Rovers knew what had happened. "Fifteen cycles ago, a disease swept through the Homefalls."

"I'm so sorry."

"It killed many, but spared those of us who were younger and the children. Only a few older survived."

Daniel remembered that time. Caring for the dying, unable to stop the high fevers or the other symptoms that appeared. The Wise Women had tried to cure it, but it had cut through them as well, diminishing their already dwindling numbers.

"Originally there were twenty-five clans." Daniel stopped, taking a deep breath. "Only five survived."

"Only…five?" The Messenger's face paled.

He nodded as he rubbed his eyes. "By the time we were able to reach the other Homefalls, most of the children had died from neglect and starvation." He closed his mind to the images threatening to overwhelm him. "They too now dwell only on the Memory Wall."

"Were there no survivors rescued?"

"None." He faced the messenger. "Although the Wellers flew in." From the soldier's puzzled expression he explained, "They were a clan once. Mark had been injured and Errl brought him here."

The memory resurfaced. Mark's bandaged face. Gem holding his hand. Taeia fighting desperately to make certain the boy kept his eyesight. The child had survived, but he bore a scar.

"Took time for us to rebuild what we had lost," Daniel continued. "Our parents would be proud of what we have accomplished." He glanced at Larry. "You have much to teach us." He needed to change the subject before his memories overwhelmed him.

"Yeah, God has handed us quite a ministry."

"The All Knowing One is wise."

"He is yes." Larry sighed. "Question is, are we up for the challenge?"

Chapter 26

"Tuleh is there anything else you want packed in the hold?" Ryk asked his daughter.

"I think I have it all." She grinned. "I left some of it on Ronia."

"You and Mikhail planning on living in our old quarters?"

"We haven't talked about it. I'm pretty sure he won't want to live in his parents' home."

"No doubt," Ryk agreed. Their old quarters would be large enough for a young couple and any future additions they might wish to make.

"I like Elaine." Her subject switch didn't surprise him.

"I do as well."

"Braiding ceremony could be a double," she suggested.

"We aren't ready for that." Besides, he wanted to wait until the Saris Homefall was recognized and Jehna became their clan chief. "Just promise me you two will attend when I do."

"We will." She moved another box into a different space, standing back to study her work. "I think that does it."

"We'll leave in two days." He couldn't believe how fast the cycle had turned. Tomorrow Tuleh would be of age.

"I want brothers and maybe a sister." She reminded him, placing her hands on hips. "You're still young enough."

"If I braid again it will be a topic of discussion."

"I wish mother were here." Her tone held sadness.

He'd known she'd bring her mother up sooner or later. "As do I." Ryk put an arm around his daughter. "She'd be proud of you, as I am."

"I doubt Mikhal will be clan chief."

"I wasn't thinking of that."

"He likes trades. I think Uncle Daniel has picked someone else."

Vaguely he remembered Lon following Daniel and Jehna around. The younger man would be a good choice as clan chief. "Whoever it will be, the choice will be wise."

"No doubt." She sat down on a box. "In some ways I'll miss being here."

"Family is family."

She nodded. "Being part of a new Homefall is exciting, but going back to Ronia, I know, is the best choice."

"With your knowledge and Mikhal's knack for trades, you'll make a formidable pair."

She laughed. "And you have knowledge to share so I suggest you get braided and start having children."

He shook his head. "That's something your mother would have said."

"Well, at least I know I inherited that from her."

~ * ~

Early the next morning, just as the sun rose, Ryk watched his cousins prepare their ships for launching the next day. The Wayas were staying behind, along with Altair and her daughter. Elaine had agreed to accompany him and he'd made certain to have guest quarters ready for her. They weren't large, but she would be comfortable enough for the short journey and their stay on Ronia.

Denebie and Roury would be traveling with his cousin and the boy followed Errl around asking questions, which were answered with more patience than Ryk thought possible. He wondered how quickly the couple would braid and have children.

"Are Elaine's quarters ready?" his daughter asked him, interrupting his musings.

Ryk nodded. "My first priority."

"Good." She laughed. "Holly seems intent on helping Aaron."

Ryk chuckled. "Per Jehna, he has no interest in the woman."

"All he cares about are trades." She shook her head. "At least for now."

"No doubt, in time, that will change."

"No doubt," she agreed. "Or when the right woman catches his eye."

"Too bad Holly isn't coming with us. We have several cousins who are looking." Forrest and Holly were staying to care for Demtrie. Altair because she wanted to continue training her daughter and get to know the man who courted her.

"Maybe another time." She wiped her forehead with her arm and looked around. "I'd say we're ready."

"We are," he agreed.

"Good. I'm helping with lunch." Tuleh hurried down the ramp and with a wave to him, weaved through the activity toward the main entrance.

"She'll be missed." Jehna stood at the bottom of the ramp.

"Means I'll have more work to do." He joined his cousin. "Uncle Daniel say anything about the clan leaders yet?"

"No."

Tanner joined them, sitting down and looking up at Jehna. "Are they coming?"

"I think so. I think they miss the desert heat."

"None of us are used to the cold and rain."

"We grew up experiencing many different climates," she reminded him.

"For short periods of time."

"We knew this Homefall would be a different experience."

"I'm beginning to not like snow."

Jehna smiled. "We'd better get used to it."

"Looks like everyone is ready." Ship hatches closed and everyone headed inside.

"Good. We can launch early tomorrow."

~ * ~

Trays of foods, fruits and vegetables waited on the table. Jehna took her place while Ryk sat down at the other end, his daughter beside him. Tuleh seemed a bit nervous. "Everything go well in the kitchen?"

"Of course," she returned, giving him a stern look.

Tradition on their Of Age Day, the one being honored helped prepare the meal the family would share. Denebie sat beside Errl and Elaine next to him. They were family, even if they hadn't braided yet.

Jehna raised her cup. "To the hands who prepared this dinner of honor, our thanks."

"Our thanks," everyone repeated.

"To the All Knowing One who provided the food, our thanks."

"Our thanks."

"In praise."

"In praise."

Food was passed, everyone taking some. Ryk had to admit the bread smelled and tasted delicious. The soup had an ingredient in it he couldn't identify. The meat tender and juicy. Conversations drifted around the table and Ryk took note of them.

Errl wanted to make a run to the Five Systems. Aaron disagreed.

The children wanted to eat and go outside to play. Rare was there a day with no work to complete.

Tanner sat next to Jehna and she gave him some meat from her plate. He gobbled it down, turning his eyes to her waiting for more.

Elaine asked, "Will it always be like this?" She indicated everyone at the table.

"When we're all at home." He sipped his cof. "Wait until the braiding ceremony."

"Aren't the messengers on Ronia?" Adrian asked.

"They are," Jehna answered. "We'll see them soon."

"Not all of us," Holly interjected.

"You can still come," Shala invited.

"You could," Forrest agreed. "I can take care of Demtrie." He glanced at the woman beside him.

"And I'm staying," Altair reminded everyone.

"I want to go to the braiding." Arissa spoke up, before a stricken expression replaced her excitement.

"She could travel with me," Jehna volunteered. "I could look after her."

"Please, mother? I'll be good," Arissa promised.

Altair hesitated. "I would talk with you in private," she told her daughter.

"That means no." Arissa pushed her plate away.

"It means we'll talk about it."

Tuleh rose and helped clear the table. Roury carried in a sweet cake while his mother poured cof for the adults and Elaine coca for the children.

Afterwards Gem and Mark gathered up the children and took them outside. Tanner joined them, his nails clicking on the floor.

Ryk finished his cof while watching Jehna and Altair quietly talking. His cousins left, each to attend whatever duties or chores needed to be done.

The women came to an agreement and Altair rose. "I'll speak with my daughter."

Jehna nodded.

He waited until the healer left before he asked. "Arissa coming with us?"

"She is. I convinced Altair it would do her daughter well to travel and no doubt Aunt Taeia may be able to spare time to teach Arissa."

"Good argument."

"Arissa needs time to be a child, not just a student."

Chapter 27

Up before dawn, a routine Jehna had gotten into while learning from Uncle Daniel, she dressed quickly and went down to the main room. On the side were bowls and cups, plus a large, covered pan of hot cereal, plus fruit, with hot cof, coca and water for her tea. Making her breakfast she sat down at the table, wondering when everyone else would be up.

Altair entered the room, her daughter rubbing at her eyes sleepily. Ushering the child to the table, Altair put a bowl of cereal and fruit along with hot coca before Arissa.

"Too early to eat," Arissa complained.

"Just a little. I don't want Jehna to worry about having food for you."

Jehna sipped her tea and kept silent. Ronia was only a few metras away, plus she'd made certain to have fruits and vegetables available for the girl to eat. As she remembered, children got hungry faster than adults.

Altair helped herself to cof and sat down. "Are you the only one leaving early?"

Jehna shook her head. "Ryk will be down shortly." She chuckled. "Tuleh slept on her father's ship last night."

"Not here?"

"I think she had a few things left to pack and probably decided it would be better to sleep there."

"Is it always like that for a braiding?"

"Can be." She hoped the healer would find out for herself one day.

"Morning," Ryk grumped pouring himself cof and then dipping into the cereal.

"Sleep much?" Jehna asked.

"Enough."

Elaine entered the room giving him a shy, warm smile. "I ate already," she explained sitting beside him.

"Did you cook this morning?" Jehna sipped more tea.

"We set the food to warm overnight. Didn't think we'd have

much time before we left."

"Good forethought."

"Anyone else up yet?"

"Most will be leaving a bit later." Jehna gathered her dishes. "I have a meeting with Uncle Daniel before the ceremony and Aunt Taeia will help Tuleh get ready."

"Since you're flying with me," she heard Ryk say as she entered the kitchen. No doubt he had a few things to explain to Elaine about the Ronia Homefall and their traditions.

Hurrying out into the still dark, she gazed at the ship the dragon had arrived in. The Shellmaster hadn't shared with them what he had found and she wondered when he would. Hopefully, it would happen within her lifetime.

Entering her ship Jehna found Tanner, Dannon and Hawk already in the hold, their preferred place to stay during the flight. Crystal slept curled up on one of the blue couches. At least they were all aboard and she didn't have to go searching for them.

Going back to the main hatch she waited as Altair escorted her daughter across the field. Kneeling down she hugged the child and spoke quietly to her. Arissa nodded and glanced at Jehna.

Rising Altair asked, "You'll take good care of her?" She handed a satchel to her.

"I will treat her as if she were my daughter."

Satisfied, yet still uneasy, or so it seemed to Jehna, the healer handed her only child into Jehna's care. "Have fun."

"I will," Arissa promised. "Where will I sleep?"

"I have a nice bed ready for you. Do you want to see?"

The child nodded.

With a glance at Altair's retreating back, Jehna closed the hatch and took the little girl to a room. To her surprise, Tanner sat there.

'Child sleepy. Need company.'

'Thank you.'

He followed them in as Altair showed Arissa where everything was. She placed the satchel on the floor as the child crawled into bed and closed her eyes. Tanner joined her, snuggling close.

'Keep her warm,' he promised.

'Call if she needs anything.'

'Yes.'

Leaving them alone she went to the control room and contacted

Demtrie. "*The Lady* ready to launch."

"Have clear stars and enjoy the braiding."

"I will."

Gently she nudged the ship up through the atmosphere and into dark space. Colored particles floated past. She easily flew through the corridor into regular space. After setting course she retreated to her quarters.

Uncle Daniel had been uneasy when he'd spoken to her the previous evening. Enough to alert her an important event could possibly happen, and it wasn't just his son's braiding. What the event might be, Jehna couldn't be sure.

~ * ~

Odd to be back on Ronia after being gone for so long. Not quite the normal homecomings she remembered. Probably because she lived on another planet and it had become as much a part of her as she was of it.

'Tanner, is Arissa awake?'

'Yes. Eating.'

'I'll be right there.'

Entering her quarters she discovered Arissa sitting on the floor with a mostly empty bowl of fruit, trying to tempt Crystal with a morsel. The Felcat sat with her tail over her paws simply watching the child.

"Are you ready, Arissa?"

She nodded and jumped up, grabbing her bowl and placing it on the counter. "Are there other children here?"

"I'm not sure." She knew a few of her cousins hadn't braided yet nor had Uncle Daniel shared much about the messengers. "How about we go see?" She offered her hand. Arissa took it and they headed for the hatch.

Once opened the desert heat invaded. She'd forgotten how hot the compound always was. Too many days and nights of cold, snow or rain on Saris.

Arissa shaded her eyes. Jehna didn't blame her. After dim days, the sun seemed too bright.

"Welcome!" Uncle Daniel waved and motioned her forward.

"Been gone too long," Jehna explained, giving the man a hug.

"Let's get inside." He picked up Arissa and carried her across the sand.

Behind her Hawk took flight, while Tanner and Dannon padded along, the leopard complaining about how the heat hurt his paws.

'Be better soon,' she heard Tanner tell the cat.

Once past the main entrance, her uncle put the child down, who gazed about completely lost.

"How's Aunt Taeia?"

"She's fine. We'll leave the child with her so you and I can talk."

"Her name is Arissa. I understand she and her mother stayed here."

"Briefly." He led the way to his home, his face not giving away his thoughts or emotions.

Her stomach knotted and she tried to calm her sudden dread. Had the clan leaders refused to recognize the new Homefall? Could be a problem if they had. Still, everyone there had worked so hard to make it successful. Jehna knew she'd fight to protect them all.

"The messengers."

Shaking herself out of her thoughts, she watched the group sitting under the trees. A little girl clung to a man, making her wonder if he was perhaps her father. Sitting beside him a woman holding a baby. Two more women, one younger than the other and two men, one of which she instantly knew.

Her uncle introduced her. "This is my cousin Jehna Talon. Arissa," he said indicating the little girl. "Our messengers," he went around giving her their names.

"We have waited a long time for your arrival." The only words she could think of to say. Arissa watched them with interest.

"So Daniel has said," the one called Larry replied. "We have quite a challenge before us."

"It may not be as difficult as you think." She shook herself, trying not to allow herself to become distracted. The woman beside him, the doctor, glanced away, as if the conversation did not involve her. Odd way to behave.

"You'll have to forgive us, Jehna and I have much to discuss."

"Of course." Larry smiled. "We'll see you later at the braiding."

He had a nice smile. "Until later," she agreed, taking Arissa's hand.

Daniel inclined his head and they moved toward his office. "What's wrong?"

"I need to talk to Aunt Taeia."

"Are those the only children?" Arissa looked disappointed.

"Until the others arrive," Uncle Daniel answered. They entered his home and he took them both into the main room. A comfortable room with curved couches and tables made of rock.

"I think you remember Arissa," he said to his wife.

"Of course. How are you?"

"Okay." She watched fascinated as the older woman moved her hands braiding a blanket. "What's that for?"

"A gift."

The girl sat on the floor lightly touching the fabric. "A gift for who?"

"That is a secret." Taeia smiled. "Would you like to help me?"

Arissa nodded.

Daniel gave his wife a smile before leading Jehna to his office, which hadn't changed. He stood and Jehna waited.

"The clan leaders insisted on having a meeting after the braiding ceremony."

She frowned, not certain if their desire to talk was good or bad. "What do you think?"

"No idea." He rubbed his eyes. "You've been attending the meetings as have I."

"Do the other clans have messengers?"

He nodded. "From what I've heard, they've been made welcome."

"Good."

"I don't know if their arrival now—"

She held up her hand. "The timing of the All Knowing One is not ours to understand."

Her uncle shook his head. "You're right."

"We can only wait to see what the outcome will be." A flash in her mind. The landing field outside her Homefall full of ships. The man she'd just met at her side. "I really need to talk to Aunt Taeia."

"A matter you aren't comfortable sharing with me."

"Not in this, Uncle."

"Understood." He sighed. "I wanted you prepared."

"You spent many cycles doing just that." Or so she hoped.

~ * ~

Arissa sat next to Taeia watching her finger weave the blanket, a few strands of fabric on the child's lap. From the archway, Jehna observed the scene, seeing for a moment another girl sitting there doing the same.

Her aunt looked up. "Finished already?"

"Yes." She sat on another couch. "I wanted to speak with you."

"Arissa," her aunt turned to the child. "In the kitchen I have a snack ready." She gave quick directions on how to get there. "You are more than welcome to it."

The little girl grinned, carefully laying the fabric on the couch and ran out.

"Children are always hungry." Her aunt gave a knowing look.

"No wonder you always had snacks ready for us." Jehna wondered how to approach her concerns. "I have the true sight."

"I suspected as much."

"You're pregnant."

"I am. The blanket is for the baby. A girl. We will share our news at the feast."

"I'll say nothing until you've announced the good news." Jehna shifted, uneasy to say the next words. "The messenger, Larry, I have had many visions with him. Beside me."

Taeia paused in her weaving. "You are certain?"

"Very."

"An interesting turn." She tucked another piece of cloth. "He arrived in the company of a woman."

"I saw." Jehna rose. "I'm not sure what to think."

"Are you not the one who always says to trust the All Knowing One?"

"Throwing my own words back at me?" she teased her aunt.

Taeia smiled. "Isn't that what good aunts do?"

~ * ~

"You wanted to see me father?" Mikhal entered his father's office.

Daniel took a deep breath. His son, who resembled the woman who birthed him. Except his eyes. His eyes were like his own. "I know you have duties before the braiding ceremony and so I'll be brief."

"Braiding ceremony is ready. Is there some last bit of advice you'd like to share?"

Direct like his mother too.

"Only that you are fortunate to have found your life mate."

"You tell that to everyone."

"So will I also share the same words with my only son."

Mikhal's eyes narrowed. "Not really what you wanted to share is it?"

Perceptive. "No." He paused deciding how best to phrase it. "Your mother is pregnant. You will have a sister."

The young man snorted. "About time."

"Oh?" He always thought Mikhal enjoyed being their only child.

"I know you had others to raise, but I always thought you should have had more children."

"You could have told us."

With a shrug he answered, "You needed to figure it out yourself."

"As I have often told you."

"Exactly."

"One question."

"Listening."

"Would you object to your cousin Lon being trained as the next clan chief?" He waited for his son's answer.

Mikhal grinned, his expression relieved. "I think Cousin Lon would make an excellent clan chief."

"I wanted to make certain before I continued his training."

"I like the trades, father. With Tuleh's help, I will make many more."

"I'm glad to hear that."

"If you'll excuse me." The young man turned to leave.

"I'm proud of you." He wanted his son to know, on this, the most important day of his life.

For a second his son became a young boy, flinging his arms around his father and holding on tightly. Daniel hugged him back. After a few moments, Mikhal pulled back, smiled, and left.

Relieved, Daniel sat down. All was ready for the braiding ceremony.

The true question, was he ready for the clan chief meeting afterwards?

~ * ~

The rest of her clan landed, slapping backs with the cousins and trading insults. Their smiles betrayed them. They were happy to be back at what had once been home.

Jehna changed from pants into her long skirt. Walking to her place near the front, her clan behind her, she noticed the messengers had been placed in the same position for the coming ceremony.

Daniel took his place, Taeia at his side. She noticed her aunt touch her stomach briefly, happy she carried a child. She hid her smile so not to alert anyone else.

Mihkal took his place, Tuleh joining him. On each of their small fingers they held a bit of green sparkle fabric.

Daniel's voice filled the area. "We are here to witness the braiding of Mikhal Talon and Tuleh Sargol."

The two young people braided each other's hair on the left side. When they finished they held hands.

"So witnessed," Daniel announced.

"So witnessed," everyone echoed.

"Time to eat!" Mark and Gem's children shouted as they headed for the loaded tables.

The adults laughed.

"Before we celebrate." Daniel stopped them. "I have an announcement to make." He took Taeia's hand. "We are expecting another child."

Stunned silence followed by hoots and whistles about the shared exciting news.

"About time," Ryk said quietly to Jehna.

"I'm happy for them." She cast a meaningful look at Elaine. "What about you?"

"You're as pushy as my daughter."

"She has a point." Uncle Daniel motioned for her to follow. "We'll talk more later." As she followed, she noticed Holly Wayas, who must decided to attend, talking with her cousin Lon Talon. They'd make a good match, she decided. Holly would be supportive for a new potential clan chief and a strong partner.

The others of her household headed to the tables for food and catching up. Jehna and her uncle entered his office. He turned on the com unit, sitting back to wait as the faces of the others appeared. Each held a stern expression and Jehna wondered if they'd already made a decision.

"There had better be a good reason for this meeting. My son braided today." Daniel glared at the other chiefs.

Andron Jovan glared back. "Your ridiculous idea."

Wayas clan leader Cameron shook his head. "I disagree with you, Andron. The reports I've gotten from Demtrie are very favorable."

"You're prejudiced, Cameron," Digon V'ianth shot back.

"Aren't you?" Rigon T'Ganth returned. The older man steepled his fingers. "I've reconsidered."

Her uncle started, leaning forward. "Reconsidered?"

"We tend to cling to the old ways simply because we thought they protected us."

"Of course, they do," Digon interrupted.

Rigon frowned at him. "Do they? Or do they keep us captive as the Arkon once did?"

Shocked silence followed his remark. Rarely did any speak of their dark past.

"You should not speak of that!" Digon retorted, anger in his tone.

Jehna listened to the exchange, keeping her silence. This meeting might decide the fate of the new Saris clan.

"We hide too much from our past," Cameron interjected. "We all know the truth and how it led to our lives as Rovers. Surely this is not hidden from those who follow behind."

"I've not hidden it." Daniel's tone reassured the other leaders. "We are too few to be concerned over what happened centuries ago."

A rebellion. A war. A fate avoided due to the mercy of the Arkon. Jehna had heard the rarely told story. They'd defended the Wise Women from attack as they'd been hired to and had been defeated. Their lives spared when their leaders promised to never to hire out their weapons again. Instead, they'd become traders of the space lanes.

"I think perhaps," Jehna spoke softly. "We are too sensitive about what our ancestors did. The decisions they made saved our lives. Perhaps we should always remember their sacrifice."

"You have a strong point," Cameron agreed. "I can see why you picked her as your successor, Daniel and as a new clan chief. She has wisdom."

"The wisdom came from Taeia." Daniel smiled briefly.

"Fortunate is the man who can hold an Arvona at his side,"

Rigon quoted a well-known saying.

"She wasn't when we braided."

No one spoke. They all knew the fate of her sister and why Taeia had been forced to take her place.

"Enough of the past." Sweeping his arm as if to brush it away, Daniel continued, "It's the future we should speak of."

"A very different one with the arrival of the messengers," Cameron agreed.

"They have much to teach us," Rigon said with respect.

Digon scowled. "I know our cousins were impressed by them."

"You have a large group," Andron teased.

"You stole the three women who came to us," Digon accused.

"The messengers didn't realize two clans shared the same Homefall." Andron grinned. "They willingly came to us since we were unable to get a ship to Charon on time."

"I don't suppose your charming smile had anything to do with it," Digon returned.

"You really should stop fighting over women." Jehna shook head. Men could have one track minds.

Digon opened his mouth, then seemed to reconsider.

"Well said," Rigon complimented. "You taught her well, Daniel. Now." He took a breath. "I think it is time to decide if Jehna would make a good clan leader." He gave her a wink. "Have you picked a clan name?"

"I have." She glanced at Daniel who nodded. "Saris."

"That's the name of your planet," Digon objected.

"It fits. We all agreed." She saw no reason to defend a decision her clan had made.

"A fitting name," Cameron agreed. "I accept Jehna Talon as the Saris clan leader."

"As do I," Rigon followed.

"As do I." Andron's support surprised her.

"You know I do." Daniel glanced at Digon.

"I don't see why not. If the Homefall fails, then it's on her head." His gaze turned to her uncle. "And yours."

One by one the clan leaders' images vanished. Jehna felt she would burst with happiness. Not only had they accepted her leadership, but the clan name as well along with the new Homefall.

"You did well." Daniel smiled at her.

"As did you." She kissed his cheek. "What say we go and enjoy the braiding feast."

He nodded. "You'll do well."

"You taught me well. Make sure you do the same with Lon. Speaking of which, I noticed Holly Wayas took a possible interest."

"We'd welcome her as part of our clan."

They left following the path to the tables set under the shade filled with family, food, and cups of cof.

The future of their Homefall was secure. She wasn't so certain about her own.

Chapter 28

Days had passed since the braiding of Mikhal and Tuleh. Jehna had waited until the entire clan was together and she took a deep breath staring into their faces, sitting around the table. "I have an announcement."

Silence fell. Even the children looked expectant.

Getting to her feet, she raised her cup. "To the Saris clan, recognized by the chiefs and our Homefall accepted."

The news took a moment for each to realize what it meant for them. A cheer exploded, with laughter and tears following.

Ryk moved to her side. "Well played, cousin."

"We had unexpected support."

"We're a clan now." He smiled at her. "With allies."

"Even so," she agreed. All the ranchers on Saris would help them if asked.

She glanced to the empty space beside her, the face of the man she felt destined for burned into her memory.

"Is the true sight ever wrong?" Ryk gently asked.

"No. Although I don't know how the All Knowing One will manage."

"Trust it will be so." His own eyes met Elaine's. She blushed. "Now I will consider braiding."

"About time," she teased.

"Past time." He moved back to his future life mate's side.

When everyone had retreated to their beds, Jehna walked out into the night. The Shellmaster's ship still hovered. He hadn't yet shared what he'd discovered. In time he would. She had only to wait. Why did she have a feeling his find would change everything?

"I don't know what truly will happen in the future," she whispered to the All Knowing One. "I trust all will work out as it should."

A whisper she could not understand tickled her ear and was quickly gone.

Tanner howled at the night sky as he and Dannon padded off to hunt. Hawk contented himself with the rafters in the barn.

Her world, at least for now, was as it should be. Jehan accepted whatever her future held for her. With or without the man who currently resided on Ronia and perhaps, one day, would be her life mate. She had only to wait on the All Knowing One's timing.

Author's Note

I laughingly called the characters in this tale a wonderful group in search of a story. I'm delighted they finally found it and that it will continue.

God's Gift originally was meant as a stand-alone. This introduces the Messengers and tells how they came to the Borders and the Five Systems. It's a prequel.

Included as well are the family trees. At a future date they may expand and you'll notice the Talons have been well developed while the others not as much. This is a series in development and it will be fun to see where it goes.

So far there are two more books planned, plus some possible future side stories.

Winter Awakening, Winter Emergence, and *Winter Moon,* tie into this series, but happen in the future.

There are several short stories which have been written and explain what happened after all the characters' adventures. Some you'll find in *Bast's Chosen Ones and other Cat Adventures.*

About the Author

Colorado based author Dana Bell writes stories about places she has lived or visited. Many feature felines. Not surprising since she has been owned by several. Taj and Esther are the current cat overlords. They are pampered and quite happy with her service.

She has written too many short stories to keep track of and is an award-winning poet. Her genres include Science Fiction, Fantasy, Horror and an unexpected story for Middle grade readers.

Hobbies include, arranging flowers, often in unusual canning jars, building, decorating doll houses, including families or singles with dogs and/or cats, making candle holders, and has, in the past, enjoyed traveling to national parks, lighthouses, and both oceans. She enjoys watching the raptor birds like hawks and eagles.

Under the pen name Belle Blukat, she writes Paranormal Romance. Her first novel, *Blood Bride,* was published a couple of years ago. Several short works are available as well.

Her imagination is endless and she is happily writing her next two to three books and submitting short stories when opportunities present themselves.

Hopefully, the cat overlords stop being jealous of the computer and allow her to write, undisturbed.

Rover Clans

Saris Clan

Name & Position — Ship — Felcat

Clan Chief: Jehna Talon — The Lady — Crystal
Her second: Ryk Sargol — Starrite — Topaz & Sapphire
Deceased life mate: Mirra
Daughter: Tuleh
Cousin Errl Weller — Clln — Linc
Brother: Mark Weller — Pride — Daze
Life Mate: Gem Morran — Cresent — Azure
Daughter: Calla
Sons: Lars, Zeke, Boas
Blood cousin: Aaron Weller — Anybody's Guess — Pint
Cousin: Adrian Colon — Ravid
Life Mate & Healer: Shala Cambrie
Demtrie Wayas — Chaser
Blood niece & nephew who are twins:
    Holly Wayas
    Forrest Wayas
Denebie
Son: Roury
Elaine
Healer: Altair Dawne
Daughter: Arissa

Shapeshifters

Black Leopard: Dannon
Wolf: Tanner
Red-Tailed Hawk: Hawk

Rover Clans

Talon Clan

Name & Position — Ship — Felcat

Clan Chief: Daniel Talon — Talon 3 — Tam
Arvona & Life Mate: Taeia — Rose
Son: Mikhal — Talon 8 — Amrac
Cousin: Lonn Talu — Aralon — Jade
Cousin: Torey Gi'an — Aralon — Jet
Blood cousin: Ryyk Talon — Talon 7 — Strip
Blood cousin: Lon Talon — Talon 9 — Sis
Uncle: Jeremy Talon — Talon 5 — Sig
Uncle: Assar Talon — Talon 4

Messengers

Major Lawrence 'Larry' Henry
Sister: Dr. Susanna Gates
Daughter: Geri
Sister: Jeanine 'Jeanie' Henry
Felcat: Leopaldi 'Leli'
Susanna fiancé: Kal Devon
Niece: Krissy
Corp. Jack Lewis
Dr. Amira Upala

Rover Clans

Jovan Clan

Name & Position — Ship — Felcat

Clan Chief Andron Jovan — Nova
Blood cousin: Ronik Jovan — Nebula
Blood cousin: Marie Jovan — Tucket
    Ronik & Marie are brother & sister
Uncle: Nicolai Jovan
Shala Cambrie was a part of this clan.

Rover Clans

V'ianth Clan

Name & Position — Ship — Felcat

Clan Chief: Digon V'ianth — Mysa
Life mate: Laurette V'ianth
Children:
Sirie
Andrew
Matthew, fostered

Rover Clans

T'ganth Clan

Name & Position — Ship — Felcat

Clan Chief: Rigon T'ganth — Tread
Life mate: Tanya T'ganth
Daughter: Tia T'ganth
Cousin: Hedron T'ganth
Cousin: Naomi T'ganth — Nels
Life mate: Axel T'ganth — Aprillette

Rover Clans

Wayas Clan

Name & Position — Ship — Felcat

Clan Chief: Cameron Wayas
Life mate: Joanna
Baby: yet to be named

More Books from
Dana Bell

Blood Bride – writing as Belle Blukat

Dr. Bertram Hoel had ignored all women he'd met until being introduced to Cira Landon at his first Science Fiction convention. Knowing he should ignore the attraction, he still takes the dangerous step to begin a relationship, aware that by doing so he is placing her life in peril.

Cira Landon wrote tales of vampire lovers unaware the handsome scientist she'd just met actually was one. Drawn to him, she finds her life threatened by an old enemy who would do anything to exact his revenge, including kidnapping her and selling her on the black market for rare blood types.

With no other options, Dr. Hoel is forced to appeal to the Elders for assistance, hoping rescue does not come too late for Cira and knowing if she is found, there is but one ancient tradition that may save her life.

Bast's Chosen Ones & Other Cat Adventures

Long ago in the land of the flooding Nile and sweeping sands, Bast created warriors called the Chosen Ones. They are her warriors. To them has been given the responsibility of protecting cats, whether on Earth or other worlds. Not always an easy task since often an ancient evil lurks, ready to pounce.

Not all felines walk in the goddess's domain. Some live in the far reaches of space, battling beside their humans or walk in lands long thought legend. Others tell their own version of human stories, walk as envoys of the creator, or appear as ghosts.

These cats walk where others dare not and do not prefer the comfort of cuddly lap warmers. Rather, they wish adventure, in present day, the past, or the far future.

God's Gift

Major Larry Henry had never expected to hear those words spoken by an alien race. Let alone one with sharp claws and fangs they used for hunting and could easily shred him, his youngest sister and her boyfriend to shreds! But when his other sister Susanna and their good friend Kal Devon disappeared from their colony, Larry and the rescue party made the astonishing discovery they weren't alone on Galilahi.

Yet Kal had hinted there were secrets being kept from the colonists. Both his friend's sister and Susanna's husband had been killed in hover accidents. The civilian and military leaders made a show of agreeing in public while Larry knew about the conflicts between them. Susanna had made discoveries about the dark fates of earlier colonies. Not to mention a jump in technology which should have taken centuries of evolution not just a few decades.

Now stranded on Galilahi with no way to relocate or return to Earth, Larry found himself wondering if the human colonists could co-exist with the feline natives or if human history would repeat itself.

Or did the God Larry believed in and trusted, have another plan none of them knew about?

Winter Awakening

Terrified shrieks reached Word Warrior's ears as he floundered up the embankment. In the gully below he saw the blood-stained snow and the dead corpse of the screaming kitten's mother. A stinky shaggy two-leg was trying to capture the youngster and he knew it couldn't be allowed to. With a battle cry born of his ancestors he charged down the hill—unaware of the high hunter lurking in the pines.

In the storm filled mountains, Anumati heard scratching at the entrance of her den. Her every instinct was to protect the three young who lay at her side. Her body tensed for battle as two howlers padded in.

World Warrior and Anumati are unaware kittens, pups and rightful prey are being stolen by strange metal monster. All that is left behind are odd, jagged paw prints of an animal they do not know.

In their world of snow and biting wind they must decide if they trust each other enough to find out the truth or if old predator-prey rules remain with no hope for change.

Winter Emergence

Kat has lived in the mountain her entire life. Going outside is allowed only to a select few, many of which never return, including her brother Ned. She doesn't want to believe he might be dead and tries every night to contact him via the coms. Silence is the only response.

Desperate to find an answer to his disappearance, Kat steals a snow cat and searches for her brother, putting the safety of everyone in jeopardy. She's joined by a cat who, for some reason, wants to come with her, and leaves once they reach the city, leaving her alone to face unknown challenges and threats for which she's not prepared.

In the city Word Warrior faces a new threat. A Striped One stalks the cats, wolves and snow ghosts killing any unfortunate enough to be caught as if they are rightful prey! He must find a way to stop the predator or all he has worked to accomplish might fail, forcing them to revert to the old laws of challenge and mate.

A new female appears bringing news of two legs, an enemy they all feared, who lived in a strange world where she had been forced to stay until she managed to escape. In fact, one was in the city and close by.

Faced with multiple threats, including worse snowstorms, Word Warrior faces the responsibility to protect their community from all dangers, knowing if he fails—they could all die.

More Books from WolfSinger Publications

The Dragon's Hoard 2 — edited by Carol Hightshoe

Welcome to realms where dragons reign, treasures abound, and every adventure leads to magic. Explore stories that spark the imagination and might just awaken the dragon within. Are you brave enough to face the dragon and claim your prize?

From the unyielding grip of ancient magics to the cunning of those who seek dragons, their treasure or both—each story weaves a rich tapestry of magic and lore.

Whether it's a battle for survival, the forging of an unlikely alliance, or a humorous twist on hoarding habits, our authors invite you to delve into realms where dragons not only hoard gold but also secrets, spells, and sometimes, even friendships. After all, in the world of dragons, not all treasures are silver and gold—some are stories waiting to be told.

The Hounds of Ardagh — Laura J Underwood

Ginny Ni Cooley never desired more than the simple life she had, living in Tamhasg Wood and using her magic to occasionally assist the folk of Conorscroft while putting up with the machinations of the ghost of her former mentor Manus MacGreeley. But her peace is shattered one night with the arrival of a lad who is fleeing a pack of red-gold hounds led by a hound-shaped demon known as Nidubh.

So much for peace and solitude. By rescuing Fafne MacArdagh, Ginny becomes wrapped in the fabric of an intrigue involving a family feud, a traitorous son, and a blood mage named Edain who is determined to keep her soul. It is she who cast a spell on Fafne's family and household and transformed the MacArdaghs into hounds.

Ginny gives Fafne her word to take him to Caer Keltora so they can report the matter to the Council of Mageborn. But Edain is determined to keep her secret and her soul intact and moves to thwart Ginny at every turn.

For Ginny Ni Cooley who has faced many bogies, dealing with a demon, a bloodmage and the Dark Lord of Annwn will be no easy task. But she will do what she must to undo Edain's spells. If not, Manus' soul will become part of Arawn's Cauldron of Doom. Ginny will become a demon's feast, and poor Fafne will join the Hounds of Ardagh.

Wee Folk and Wise: A Fairies Anthology
– edited by Deby Fredericks

All over the world, fairy tales are told.
There are big fairies and little fairies.
Ugly fairies and pretty fairies.
Wise fairies and silly fairies.
Sweet fairies and scary fairies.

Seventeen authors share their own fantastic fairy tales in this magical collection. What kind of fairy will you meet here?

Infinity – Ted Pennella

In the distant future, when peace between humanity and the artificial intelligences their ancestors created has been settled, Conrad Conner tries to live a quiet and unassuming life in orbit about Jupiter on the city-station Socrates' Odyssey. When Conner's attempt to create a prototypical communication artificial for use by the Sol-Humana Confederation's Stellar Fleet gets derailed by the attempted murder of the very artificial he's created, his life spirals into a mad flight back to Earth to try and save at least his sister's children, if not his sister herself. Past failures and heartaches resurface as seemingly unconnected dots become a plot by the First Admiral to steal not just power over the Confederation, but a secret Conner holds within himself.

A secret not even Conner knows about.

Flatlanders - Mike Sherer

Young theoretical physicist Mickey Haiku has fallen into Eden's trap. She is a much smarter scientist who is intent on saving her own dimension by destroying his. Unbeknownst to either, beings from several yet higher dimensions have their own strategies. This sends the mixed-up pawns off on a wild odyssey through a dozen weird, twisted dimensions. As if this hyper-dimensional odyssey isn't challenging enough for Mickey, he has the additional difficulty of embarking on this whacko tour as a (pregnant!) female. Which means Eden is stuck in Mickey's body. The two are soon forced to cooperate since each holds the other's body hostage.

The strangest relationship this side of the 11th dimension develops between the two.

Fires of Rapiveshta: Book Three: A Familiar's Tale
— Verna Mckinnon

With Obsydia's chaos growing and more kingdoms falling under her control, Runa, Mellypip and their friends scramble to find a way to stop her from discarding her mortal form and claiming their world in the name of her Eternal Father Ahridum and plunging it into a never-ending age of darkness and evil.

The dragons of Rapiveshta are awakened from their long slumber by Obsydia's attempt to steal the egg that holds the unborn dragon who will become the next leader of the dragon clans. The egg is given to Runa's grandfather to protect it. When it hatches, Mellypip finds himself bonded to the baby dragon as her guardian.

As Obsydia reaches the climax of the ritual that will burn away her mortality, Runa, Opaline and Panthara find themselves captured to be used as sacrifices. Will the Gate of Souls claim Runa and Mellypip as the Winged Fey have foreseen? Or will the Fires of Rapiveshta and those chosen to be the Scions of Light be able to save them and their world.

Borne in the Blood — edited by Carol Hightshoe

Delve into the mysterious and powerful world of blood in "Borne in the Blood"

This collection of enthralling stories explores the multifaceted essence of blood—as a symbol of life, a medium of magic, and a bond of kinship. From the chilling tale of a minstrel haunted by a spectral king to the whimsical account of a vampire ice cream vendor, each story weaves a unique narrative around the theme of blood. Encounter a woman whose body bizarrely intertwines with metallic elements, and follow a girl's journey as she confronts her isolation due to her heritage. Feel chills as those who were wronged reach across the years to have their final revenge on the blood descendants of those who oppressed them.

Shifters, Vampires, Witches, and other ordinary and extraordinary folk—all bound together by that which they carry in their blood.

These tales will transport you through a spectrum of emotions, from the depths of fear to the heights of fantasy, as you unravel the mysteries and power that lie within the blood.

Proceeds from sales of Borne in the Blood will be donated to the Multiple Myeloma Research Foundation – themmrf.org/

Space Brides, LLC – edited by Dana Bell

Tired of those lonely dark nights? No one in your settlement suitable? We are here to help! We will help you find the bride or husband to keep you company, raise your children, and be your partner building a dream together. Contact us directly and give us your specifications. Success guaranteed.

In this collection of 15 testimonials read about the challenges and triumphs of some of our clients as they found love on the frontier of space.

From aliens to vampires, we brought these couples together and together they found acceptance and love—each in their own way.

A man with three kids finds an unexpected match in the brother of the woman he had contracted to marry when she runs away.

A woman running away from an abusive marriage finds acceptance and respect with a colony group that marries everyone to everyone in order to ensure they know they belong to a family.

A woman constantly rejected because of her skin color and origins finds acceptance and love with a wounded soldier.

Even though we encourage absolute honesty in your profile and correspondence with your potential spouse—many people don't. However, like some of the testimonials you'll read here; they still manage to expand their horizons—together.

Contact or walk into any of our offices 24/7. We are here to help you find that special someone and start a new future!

Other conditions apply.
Please ask for more information before contract is drawn up and signed.

The Dragon's Hoard – edited by Carol Hightshoe

Dragons are well known for their hoards—but not all hoards are created equal.

A young dragon starts his hoard with some very precious gifts.

One dragon shares her complaints about taxes with a friend as they wait for a lunch delivery.

Another dragon defends her most precious treasures against a group of greedy goblins.

And yet another may hold the solution to saving the Earth after a devastating apocalypse in his collection of bottled treasures.

In addition to the normal gold, silver and jewels here you will find dragons who collect many different treasures. 25 storytellers invite you to enter *The Dragon's Hoard* and share the treasures within.

And more – check out our books at
www.wolfsingerpubs.com

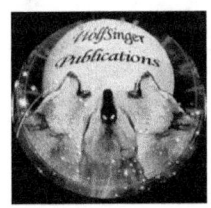